Just from the walk from the train station to the smith's, her skirts were covered in dust. And her boots—she'd never had dirt in those buttonholes before. Thankfully, Captain Peele hadn't picked her up at the station. Before she met him, she needed a bath, a bed, and a fresh dress.

"You're no social club girl, either." More hitting sounded.

Moving, she cupped her hand over her eyes again to shield the sun for a better look. The smith intrigued her. "What do you mean social club?"

He chuckled low and soothing, like the rumbling of rain. Maisie blushed with realization. *A house of ill repute.* Her mother had warned her about places like that. She guarded against them in the Watch and Warn Society. Maisie doubted they had the old "W&W," as she called it, here in Wyoming Territory.

Pointing with his hammer, he paused. "You look like a woman of class and distinction, and I cannot figure out why you would be wandering the streets of Wylder."

The timbre of his voice thrilled her. She couldn't tell if he was teasing or being serious. Something about his friendliness tugged at her heart. A bead of happiness burst through her. But she was meant for Christopher. Nevertheless, a smile stole across her lips. "I'm actually looking for Captain Peele. Do you know him?"

Praise for Amey Zeigler

"A feisty Boston Brahmin and a scarred Civil War vet won my heart in Amey Zeigler's *WYLDER BRIDE*, a skillful retelling of one of literature's most famous unrequited love stories."

~Anna M. Taylor, author

~*~

"Amey Zeigler's *WYLDER BRIDE* is everything you'd want from a historical western romance. Wonderfully believable characters and an action-packed plot make this a delight to read! Well done and highly recommended!"

~Sarita Leone, award-winning author

~*~

"A beautiful story of determination, of a love made through words, and a heart knowing what the mind takes longer to realize."

~ April Hollingworth, author of
The Candi Reynolds Series

~*~

"*WYLDER BRIDE* is hands-down a story you shouldn't miss. Amey Zeigler gives us a romance with heart and passion for real love."

~Kim Turner, author of WYLDER HEARTS

Wylder Bride

by

Amey Zeigler

The Wylder West

Wylder Bride

Cover Art by *Tina Lynn Stout*

The Wild Rose Press, Inc.
PO Box 708
Adams Basin, NY 14410-0708
Visit us at www.thewildrosepress.com

Publishing History
First Edition, 2022
Trade Paperback ISBN 978-1-5092-4068-5
Digital ISBN 978-1-5092-4069-2

The Wylder West
Published in the United States of America

Dedication

For my mother,
who has the courage of a frontier woman

Chapter 1

Boston, 1879

Maisie Brinley refused to descend the stairs for dinner. Her mother invited the stuffy, self-absorbed, yet wealthy, Ralph Pope to dine tonight. They hadn't invited him to discuss the politics of moving to the gold standard, either. No, this dinner party would end in a marriage proposal.

Perhaps he would arrive tonight on his newly acquired bicycle all the way from the financial district, rebuilt nearly seven years ago after the fire of 1872. When she last saw him at the Boston Common earlier in the spring, he looked so silly balanced upon the two-wheeled contraption.

Tying a knot in her sheets, Maisie stifled a laugh against her hand. Leaning out the third floor window to view the other stately brick mansions with mansard roofs along the South Slope of Beacon Hill, she dropped the lengthy rope ladder made from her tightly woven bed sheets to the brick streets below. How would she manage the climb in her skirts? Thankfully, her kid leather boots were sturdy.

"What are ye doing there?" Cara O'Donnell asked from behind.

Maisie glanced over her shoulder. "I'm running away." She wanted trees and wilderness, not people and houses.

"And just where do ye think ye'll go this time?" Cara brushed back a strand of red hair and tucked it into her cap. Thrusting her chin into the air, she planted a fist on her thin hip. "Ye have no place to go. Ye'll just be dragged home by Constable Higgins again. Now get away from the window before ye fall and break yer neck, and then what would yer mother do with ye?" She snagged the bedsheets and pulled them from the window, untying the knots and shaking her head. "Bless me, Miss Maisie, if ye aren't a handful of trouble. Now I have to rewash the linens."

Along with her Irish brogue, Cara's grin always brought a smile to Maisie's own lips. Only two years separated them. Maisie never gloated over her superiority in her age or station. She narrowed her eyes. "I could still climb down the drainpipe and run off." Ever since they were installed, the thought tempted her. "But then I would miss you, my dear friend." She sighed. "Don't worry. I'll help you wash the bedding. It's my fault they're all soiled." Cara was right. She had no place to go.

"Bah, ye know yer mother wouldn't permit ye doing the wash. Besides, ye don't know how!" Done with separating the sheets, Cara set to work remaking the bed with fresh linens. "Now, come away from the window and dress for dinner. Ye must dine with Mr. Pope tonight, miss. He's a very good match."

"You sound like my mother." Frowning, Maisie straightened the hem of her tailored, drop-waist cuirass bodice and studied the pink damask wall coverings surrounding the open window. Horses' hooves clapped on the cobblestone and brick streets below. Bells rang from their harnesses. A breath of chilled smoke from the neighboring stacks invigorated her. "Perhaps he's a match for some other stuffy, straitlaced debutante but not me." She couldn't imagine having a blissful home full of laughter, love, and warmth with him. The only thing underneath Ralph's ribs was a bank account.

"And I might add, he's one of the last bachelors in all New England whom ye haven't snubbed." Shaking a finger, Cara pitched her eyebrows.

True. Maisie had a tongue in her head and a brain that powered it—much to her mother's disapproval. Cara was right. Maisie sent more than her fair share of suitors running with a few short words. Her mother must be getting desperate if she considered Ralph Pope—someone whose mother wasn't part of the Boston elite. What horrors! Maisie rolled her eyes at her mother's snobbery. "I suppose I must at least eat."

"There's a good girl." Cara finished folding the sheets. "Now come and get dressed."

Moving away from the open window, Maisie removed her arms from the oppressive long sleeves. Even in chilly early May, her clothing suffocated her. In fact, everything about Boston suffocated her.

Cara removed the day bodice and laid it on the four-poster bed. She slid the evening bodice with shorter sleeves over the corset. "You'll look beautiful in this bodice, miss. I'm sure the honorable Mr. Pope will be taken with you."

"That is precisely what I wish to avoid." Maisie slid her hands through the delicately stitched sleeve hole and adjusted the lace around her bertha collar.

"Don't ye want to get married?" At the foot of the bed, Cara tugged at the spiral lacings up the back of the dark purple silk faille.

Maisie stood in front of the wardrobe. "Of course I do. Just not to any of the men my parents want for me. I want a real man—one with gumption, grit, and passion." She ran her hands down the front drape of her dress, grateful she didn't have to change her skirts for dinner. Getting in and out of the bustle, the crinoline, and the bum pad took no small amount of work for the both of them. "What happened in the last one hundred years that turned all the Boston men—the firebrands of the Revolution—into wet, wool socks?"

"What do ye think?" Cara turned her toward the looking glass embedded in the wardrobe.

The dress was no Worth gown, but Maisie had to admit the image pleased her.

A knock sounded on the door behind her.

"Yes?" Maisie turned to see who entered.

Mother bustled into the room with the rustle of silk. Her evening dress was the picture of a Boston socialite. White lace gathered around her shoulders. Her silhouette formed an hourglass with the help of yards of skirt fabric bunched and draped around the skirt. Silk flowers dotted the gown. "You look beautiful, Margaret. The dark violet complements your complexion and dark hair perfectly." She stopped in front of the mirror to smooth her dress and soothe her fading dark locks into place on top of her head.

"Thank you." Maisie wrinkled her nose at her use of her Christian name. No one but her mother called her Margaret. Even Cara called her Miss Maisie. Sometimes Maisie felt like Grandpa's Revolutionary muzzle-loader hanging over the mantel in the dining room, beautiful but useless—decoration only. Since her coming out at sixteen, she'd done little more than be a glass-headed doll for Mother to parade about.

"Good heavens!" Mother crossed the room in a flurry of lavender scent. "Who left the window open?" She shut the sashes, drowning out the sound of the street below. "I hate the dust and the noise. Really, Margaret, you shouldn't keep the windows open." Mother's forehead creased with wrinkles.

Maisie rolled her eyes. Her mother loved to worry. She worried about getting trampled by horses, or getting her skirts caught in the wheels of her carriage, or whether novels would spoil Maisie's brain, or if she'd catch pneumonia or measles—the latter was perhaps because Maisie's baby sister died of the disease. Mother always kept a lock of the baby's hair in her locket around her throat. Her primary concern was to marry off Maisie to someone worthy of her station.

Her mother clutched a scented hanky to her chest. "Please remember to be civil tonight." The crease marred her brow again. "We are running out of eligible bachelors. Now, Ralph just returned from London so he doesn't know about all your other flaws yet. If we can secure an engagement—"

"My flaws?" Maisie's throat tightened. Mother used her charm to win allies to her causes but reserved little tact for their conversations.

"He hasn't heard the gossip." Clutching the pearls at her neck, Mother raised her eyes to the ceiling. "Oh, Margaret, if only you knew how important your reputation was, you'd guard it more closely."

A fire stoked in Maisie's heart. Heat burned her cheeks. "If you're referring to the termination of my engagement with Harold Peabody—" Jewels adorned the fake hair pieces in her mother's hair. She meant business tonight.

"I don't want to hear about it." Mother brushed back faded, pewter hair which had fallen loose from her pompadour and tugged on Maisie's bodice. "I know you had your reasons for ending it, but to be known as a Jilting Jessy! You've made men skittish. They want a woman they can trust."

Maisie crossed her arms. That was not what Harold Peabody wanted.

"What I'm trying to say is, Ralph might be our last hope for marrying anyone suitable. You're twenty-six, Margaret, and you're not getting any younger."

Emotion built in her chest. Maisie dropped her jaw. Her mother talked about her as if she were milk curdling in the sun. True, all the young ladies from finishing school were married, and most even had children of their own. Maisie was the last of her circle of friends to marry. She didn't need it rubbed in her face.

Cara quietly bowed and backed from the scene.

Narrowing her eyes, Maisie faced her mother. She thrust out her jaw. "I just want a man who is a real man, not a banker, not a business man, but one who stands straight and tall because he hasn't cheated the world to climb to where he is. I want someone who works hard with his hands, who creates beauty, and who understands craft. I doubt I will find those in Ralph."

Mother tucked in her lips. Tears formed in the corners of her eyes. "If this doesn't end in a proposal, Margaret, I don't know where else to turn."

Maisie faced the glass again, plucking at her lace collar. "Turn to God." Perhaps she meant it a little flippantly, or perhaps not. God was always her friend as long as He allowed her to do what she wanted.

Mother raised a single brow. "Perhaps I shall."

Maisie picked up the latest print edition of the newspaper. "I want to do something heroic or make a new discovery. Did you hear they found a geyser out west that erupts at the same time every day? Amazing, isn't it? I read about it in the *Boston Courier*. Or here is a man who foiled a bank robbing. How exciting to get your name in the paper for doing something so heroic."

Her mother furrowed her eyebrows. She pinched her lips together. "Shameful. You should only be mentioned in the newspaper when you are born, when you are married—soon hopefully—and when you die, which will be sooner than you think if you do not make yourself pleasing to Mr. Pope."

Her mother's straight mouth and serious tone sobered Maisie. "I will try to be nice to Mr. Pope, but if he brings up his bicycle, I will laugh."

Lifting her chin, Mother puffed out her chest. "I mean it, Margaret. This is your last chance before I am forced to take drastic measures. Behave tonight at dinner—or else!" Her mother slammed the door behind her.

Maisie lifted the papers again with a burdened heart. People were so free out west—no bankers, no expectations, and no Mr. Pope. She just had to figure out how to get there.

****

Bent over his forge, Cyrus Haddock rotated to the slack tub and quenched the purple steel. Steam rose from the limed water. Near him, the coal forge burned bright orange amid the damp, pea-sized coke built up around the heart of the flame. A huge chimney swept the smoke up into the sky. The mid-morning sun created a patchwork of yellow on the dirt floors of his shop.

Though snow still hid in the shadows outside in the chilly, late Wyoming spring in Wylder, sweat poured off his brow. Cyrus focused on tempering his steel. He loved to tune out everything and focus on creating. Today he repaired an action for a revolver. Often, he lost himself in his own thoughts and relived the battle scenes of his youth in the War Between the States.

He wiped the sweat from his scarred brow. Even after sixteen years, he swore the rippled part of his face still felt more sensitive to heat.

All alone, he sank deep into his thoughts while he allowed the steel to cool. At his bench, he picked up the action of the revolver he replaced after the firing pin broke. Although he loved repairing broken guns, creating them satisfied him more. Organizing raw materials and making something never before seen, never before created—a unique piece—was what he lived for. Grips with pearl-accented handles, carving wood and antlers into hunting scenes, or mere decorative designs were his specialty. He loved silver handles for their sheer beauty. The racks at the front of his shop displayed rows of his work. Each one was unique. Each one was a piece of art.

"You the gunsmith?"

The voice broke his concentration. He lowered the steel. The six men must've entered while he focused on the detail of his work. "That's what the sign says over the door." Keeping the scarred side of his face away from the visitors, he wiped his hands and tucked his polishing cloth into his leather apron. "How can I help you gentlemen?"

He used the term "gentlemen" broadly. These men looked like seedy ranch hands from a ranch up north—illiterate, uncouth, lazy, and brash. Their teeth were yellow. Their hair hung in greasy ropes near the edges of their unshaven jaws. Their clothes looked slept in and unwashed. Even over the smoke of the coal forge, he smelled their unseemly body odor—a familiar odor.

The foremost among them cocked his head.

"Gambell?" Cyrus blinked in the dim light of the shop. A flash of heat hit his chest. The last time he'd seen Private Gambell was on the battlefield. "You deserted the Northern Army. I had orders to shoot you on sight."

Gambell split open his mouth in a wide, toothy, and insincere grin. Cyrus shuddered.

Gambell spit in the dirt floor. "I thought I recognized you. You called me a coward once."

"Only once? I couldn't sworn I said it at least a dozen times." Cyrus narrowed his eyes to get a good look at Gambell's friends. They looked like the type of men who frequented the social clubs and saloons more than the respectable places in town. "What are you doing here?"

One slouched, tucking his hands into the pockets of his leather vest.

Another possessed the greasiest hair. From his dusty bowler hat to his too-tight jacket to his unpolished boots, he shone with an oil sheen.

Gambell whisked back his shoulder-length, straw-colored hair. "We're looking for six-shooters."

"Yeah."

Cyrus shot his gaze to the third friend who talked too loud.

"Word on the street is that you make the most accurate guns."

This one tapped his foot incessantly on the dirt floor and thrummed his fingers on his worn chaps. He reminded Cyrus of a coil wound too tight. With the slightest flick, he would jump into action.

Cyrus, unmoved by the possible sincere flattery, refocused on situating the firing pin into the action. His rifles earned legendary status in Wyoming Territory. "I'm afraid my guns are not for the likes of you." He arched his unscarred brow. They'd probably use them for nefarious purposes.

Gambell shook his head. "I'm offering whatever price you ask for your rods."

Tilting his head a little toward him, Cyrus stared with his good eye. "I'm sorry. You can get a 'rod' in Cheyenne. I'm sure some sucker there would love to take your money. I create art, not rods."

His face contorted. "You must be some kind of stupid."

"Yes, I suppose I am." He sighed and fingered his hammer. He yearned to return to work.

The round-faced ranch hand held out a stack of greenbacks.

An intense aroma surrounded him. Cyrus coughed to blow away the stink.

"Backed by gold, brother."

Again, Cyrus shook his head.

"You just greedy?" Talks-Too-Loud shook his head.

"Of the greatest sorts. Greed for a reputation of

goodness and quality. Now if you'll allow me, I'll return to my work." Sitting at his bench, he searched for a scrap of paper. He had an idea for a pastoral scene he wanted to sketch before squelching the forge for the night. He preferred to return to his little homestead before sunset. Although, on occasion, he often worked late in his shop and slept under his bench. No one waited for him at his lonely house. Those three acres seemed like miles of solitude.

"You're a foolhardy man." Gambell stepped in his direction.

"Again, I agree with you." Although he focused on his workbench, Cyrus watched him from the corner of his eye. He hoped they'd give up and go away. He arranged his tools on the wood.

A man with a red beard stepped from the back. "If you won't give them to us, we'll take them by force."

"You can try." Cyrus remained seated. He didn't even arch a brow at their threats.

"You can't stand against six men." Talks-Too-Loud's whole body shook.

Placing his tools on the bench, Cyrus sighed. His patience ran out. Standing, he faced the men. "Kindly leave my establishment."

The men stepped back.

"What's wrong with his face?" asked the smelly one with dark, stringy hair and a mustache standing in the back—Stinky.

Red-Beard spit tobacco juice into the dirt floor. "Did a cow step on your face when you was born?"

A chuckle rose from the men.

Greasy sneered. "Or did a wolf mangle your face?"

Inhaling, Cyrus slid his hand around a revolver

sitting on the bench. "You shouldn't have asked that."

The ranch hands drew their sidearms.

Calmly, Cyrus aimed and one by one shot each gun out of their hands without so much as nicking their fingers with a bullet.

Talks-Too-Loud dropped his jaw and pounced on his gun.

Narrowing his eyes, Red Beard swore.

Greasy licked his lips.

Slouchy just bent to pick it up, real slow, with his gaze still on Cyrus.

In the blink of his eye, Cyrus reloaded and shot the dirt floor near the tips of Slouchy's fingers. In the fastest move he'd made since he entered the shop, Slouchy stood straight.

Shaking his head, Gambell bent to retrieve his gun.

Again, Cyrus let out a warning shot near Gambell's hand. "See how this goes? You retrieve your guns, and I'll shoot. I've got enough ammo here to do this all day." He pointed to the cartridges stacked on the windowsill above his bench.

Gambell spit on the dirt floor. "Get him."

Red Beard, Greasy, and Talks-Too-Loud circled Cyrus.

At close range, he worried about wounding them. Cyrus didn't want to kill the men—just teach them a lesson. He stepped back along the bench. Tossing the revolver along his four-hundred pound mill, Cyrus reached for his two-pound hammer. He walloped Red Beard in the stomach.

He doubled over and stumbled out the door.

Greasy grabbed him from behind.

Cyrus head-butted him in the face then jabbed him

in the stomach with the hammer.

Greasy landed face first into the smoldering fire. "Ahhhh!" Grasping his face, he raced out the door with soot covering his shoulders, his collar on fire.

The four men left circled Cyrus. Gambell spit through his yellow teeth. "You should've just given us what we asked for."

Cyrus shook his head. "I see no need to acquiesce to mob mentality."

All at once they rushed him.

With brute strength, Cyrus knocked Gambell in the jaw with the hammer. He hit Slouchy on the right shoulder, and Stinky and Talks-Too-Loud he hit along their left sides like he was swinging a club.

Gambell spit out two teeth. He swiped his mouth. "You haven't seen the end of this." Blood dribbling from his mouth, he and his companions stumbled out the door.

Cyrus raised the hammer in a sword salute to the now-empty shop. No doubt those ruffians would be back. He sighed. *Drat*. Now he'd have to install iron bars over the windows.

Chapter 2

Holding her breath, Maisie stepped into the spacious sitting room with a pair of Belter-style mauve, damask, upholstered canopy sofas facing each other in front of the hearth. In the spring chill, the fireplace roared. Mounted above the wooden, dentil mantel was Great-Grandpa Benjamin Shaw's flintlock musket, all polished brass and wood. Next to it, his powder horn carved with scenes from the Revolutionary War hung on a peg alongside a leather ammunition bag. Over a hundred years passed since her family stood against the most powerful, most numerous, most disciplined army the tyrant-king ever put to field and won. In her family, only stories and this musket remained of their valor. Maisie lifted her chin. Their rebellious blood ran through her veins.

Grandpa Shaw, in his eighties, smoked a clay pipe, much to Mother's dismay, and sat in a high-backed, tufted, pink ornate wingback chair near the fireplace, no doubt to hide the stench of his tobacco from Mother. His white brows met in the middle of his wrinkled forehead as he stared into the flames.

Placing a hand on the Federal-style mantel, Maisie sighed. This dinner party wasn't the first or the last time her parents would set her up. She stared at the musket. The sunlight from the tall windows flanking the chimney illuminated the reddish wood and the surrounding brass. So beautiful, so powerful, yet for the rest of its life it would be here guarding the mantel—on display, useless, and not living up to its potential. She faced Grandpa. "We're having company for dinner."

He raised his cloud-like eyebrows. "So I heard." He puffed more. His teeth clinked on the clay. "You know, Lafayette himself gave that musket to my grandfather Benjamin Shaw."

"You've told me the story a thousand times, Grandpa." Somehow she doubted the family lore.

He removed his pipe and pointed at the flintlock. "This gun shot Redcoats at the Battle of Bunker Hill."

She rolled her eyes. Every time he shared the story, he elaborated even more. Was Old Ben even in that battle? She turned and ran a finger along the smoothed wood of the barrel. Tiny nicks marred the wood. She would never correct Grandpa.

"My grandfather kept the British at bay as they stormed Bunker Hill. Only they didn't storm Bunker Hill. They stormed Breed's Hill." He wheezed and coughed.

Maisie didn't know who mixed up the hills and build a defensive redoubt on the wrong spot, but such was the way with war. Communication was poor. She dropped her hand from the mantel. "I'm afraid its glory days are behind us." She sighed.

Grandpa Shaw clenched his teeth on his pipe again. "That's what you think. That gun could still shoot. You'll never know when it would come in handy someday." He winked. "I've left it to you in my will."

Maisie raised her eyebrows. Giving a woman a gun? A sense of pride burst through her. Grandpa thought she could handle it. He believed in her rebel blood.

A knock sounded on the front door.

Maisie's heart sank. Dread grew in her stomach. "He's here."

Grandpa scowled again. "I should've asked to have dinner in my room." He stood on shaky legs and held out his elbow.

Maisie took his outstretched arm. "You and me both, Grandpa," she said under her breath because he couldn't hear her.

He escorted her to the vestibule.

Her father stood on the marble floor in front of the great, leaded-glass door with Ralph Pope.

Mr. Pope removed his hat and his top coat and handed them to the butler. Light reflected off his bald head from the gas chandelier above.

Despite his love of bicycles, his exercise had done nothing to slim his figure. His rounded, bloated body hovered over skinny legs. He was a hot air balloon in a suit. At least he smiled pleasantly under his handlebar mustache. A large gap separated his two front teeth.

"So grateful you can join us for dinner." Mother swept into the front vestibule with a rustle of silk and a breath of lavender. She took both of Mr. Pope's hands. "Margaret has been eagerly awaiting this dinner engagement."

Mother turned and gave Maisie a warning with her eyes.

Maisie resented the lie and bit her lip to keep from saying the truth. Heat smoldered within her, despite the shorter sleeves of her dress.

Bowing, he greeted Maisie with a kiss to her hand.

"Shall we?" Mother took Father's arm. "Ralph,

dear, Margaret would love for you to escort her to her chair."

Mr. Pope's smile grew bigger, if it were possible, and held out his elbow for Maisie. Letting go of Grandpa, she took Mr. Pope's elbow and turned away so he wouldn't see her grimace. Did her mother have to be so obvious?

Father took the head of the table. His gaze, vacant since his service in the war, swept the table. Luckily, Maisie's brother, Andrew, ran the family importing business now.

Poor Mr. Pope tried hard. He slid out her chair and tucked her under the tablecloth with impeccable manners, only stepping on her dress a few times in the ordeal.

He sat across from Maisie, his back toward the fireplace.

Jenkins helped Mother sit opposite her husband.

Grandpa Shaw parked beside Mother on her right hand side.

After her father said grace, he signaled to Jenkins to command the soup to be brought in on Mother's bone china. "I've heard you joined the recently established Bicycle Club, Pope."

"Oh, yes." Mr. Pope unfolded the napkin and placed it on his lap.

Jenkins slid a shallow bowl of soup under Mr. Pope's nose.

Ralph dipped and sniffed. His chest swelled with the inhalation. "This smells delightful."

Maisie balked at Mr. Pope's breech in manners. If her mother had caught Maisie sniffing soup like a hound, she would've rapped her knuckles for sure. She slid her gaze to check her mother's reaction.

Mother only smiled and delicately picked a spoon from the lineup of silverware. "Thank you. It's spring leek soup. Do eat."

He grabbed a spoon and dug in. "Bicycling is wonderful exercise." He slurped his soup. "I believe everyone should try it. Riding every day helps stabilize the core muscles. My legs feel stronger and more efficient. Wonderful invention—the bicycle."

"Did you ride your bicycle here, then?" Maisie couldn't help herself. She blinked in earnest expectation and scooped up a spoonful of soup. The warmth coated her mouth. The mildness of the leeks reminded her of spring.

Her mother scowled.

Grandpa hid a smile.

Her father ate soup.

With his spoon in mid-air, Mr. Pope frowned, lowering his hand. "I, uh, no. I bicycle for hobby sport, not for transportation." He smiled, slid his gaze to her mother, and slurped the spoon.

"And how are the banks doing, Mr. Pope?"

Mother shot Maisie a warning glance over her bowl. Maisie refocused on her soup.

"Not good, not good. Bankers talk of going off the gold standard." He tsked his tongue and shook his head.

"Is that not a good thing?" Maisie asked. "If a limited amount of gold can only be held by the rich, what then shall the poor do?"

"The poor should be happy to serve us." Mr. Pope smiled and wiped his mouth with the linen napkin. "We give them wages, do we not? Let the rich pay the poor for the privilege of work."

What rubbish! Maisie raised her eyebrows but said nothing. She caught her grandfather's eye across the table. Another spoonful went into her mouth.

He shook his head.

Maisie wiped the corners of her lips. "So we hoard all the money, then dispense it to feel generous when we need work done? Wouldn't it be better to allow all men the same opportunity to make money?"

"Not everyone has the brains for business." Passing his napkin across his forehead, Mr. Pope dropped it to the floor. "I'm sorry," he said to Jenkins. "Could I trouble you to get me another?"

Jenkins's eyes grew large.

What a strange man, who in one breath apologized to servants but rejected a system that could help him get out of their present state of poverty?

"Besides." Pope sniffed. "Women should not talk about such things. Financial affairs are for men. You don't have to worry your sweet, little head about such matters."

Maisie bit her lip and stirred her soup. "I always believed that if you give a woman knowledge, she teaches generations. When you teach a man, he uses that knowledge to further his own interests."

Ralph Pope lowered his spoon. "I don't understand your last statement."

She arched her eyebrow and jutted out her chin. He paid handsomely for his hand-tailored suit. "I see by your lifestyle you surely agree."

A spoon clattered.

Her mother sat open-mouthed at the end of the table.

Even Father furrowed his eyebrows.

With grave disappointment in his eyes, Grandpa shook his head. Maisie's heart burned. Heat rushed to her cheeks and ears. She sat in silence for the rest of the meal.

The only conversation at the table consisted of Mother and Mr. Pope exchanging small talk.

After dinner, the men left to drink port in the library.

Clutching her skirts, Maisie thundered upstairs.

"Margaret, dear." Her mother waved a scented handkerchief. Her eyes grew large. She trembled.

Maisie halted on the landing. She gripped the ornate wooden banister. This request couldn't be good. Dread grew in her stomach.

With one hand pinching her skirts, Mother marched up with stairs and met her on the landing. "Mr. Pope would like to talk with you in the library. Privately." She emphasized the last word.

After dinner, she hoped Mr. Pope wanted nothing more to do with her. "No, thank you. Mr. Pope can have nothing to say to me in private. Tell him I had a headache and begged to return upstairs." Lifting her skirts, she mounted a stair.

"Margaret." Mother tugged at her elbow. "You will listen to Mr. Pope. He has come all the way from New York to speak to you."

"I don't want to speak to him."

Mother wrung her hands. Her shoulders slumped. "You are twenty-six and not getting any younger. You have a reputation of jilting men. No eligible bachelor in Boston wants to marry you. Do you want to be an old maid? Passed over? Left over? Forgotten? Like Aunt Lucinda?"

A lance pierced Maisie's heart. She descended the stairs. Aunt Lucinda was the butt of the Boston Brahmin's gossip and jokes. Her father's sister far outlived her wits. She owned a pet kinkajou and filled her house with stuffed animals situated under glass, bell-shaped domes. Maisie didn't know which she hated the most—the frozen crow on a branch or the taxidermy squirrel holding a nut.

Mother's accusations stung, but the rumors of jilting cut her to the core. If only her mother knew what happened, but instead of asking her or even listening to the truth, her mother preferred to stay ignorant of the whole affair.

"And no insulting remarks." Mother dragged Maisie into the library, shoved her inside, and closed the sliding oak doors behind her.

Mr. Pope stood staring at the painting above the desk.

Trapped, Maisie lifted her chin. She knew just what a private conversation entailed. She'd been proposed to at least a dozen times. With each one, her mother held such high hopes. And at least eleven of those times crushed her.

Clearing his throat, Mr. Pope faced her.

Sweat glistened on his bald forehead. Against the light of the window, his balloon shape grew even more apparent.

Mr. Pope crossed the room. He took her hand.

His pale palm was moist. Maisie fought herself to keep from recoiling from his touch.

"I have known your family for years now." He swallowed visibly. "I have grown fond of you, despite your outspoken ways. I hope you will join me in New

York this spring. I would love to introduce you to my family. A friend of mine is renaming the old Gilmore's Gardens to Madison Square Gardens in a ceremony this May, and I'd love for you to come." He raised his eyebrows and lifted his rounded chin.

His insult about women not talking about finances still rang in her mind. "Would we ride your bicycle down, or would we pay some poor fellow for the privilege to take us?" Maisie bit her lip as soon as the words left her mouth. She finally said too much.

His smile fell. "I am just a joke to you?"

Heat flashed her face. "No, I—"

"I pity you, Miss Brinley. You are the woman no man wants. And now I know why. You cannot hold your tongue. You are most unladylike. I forgave the remark at dinner, but this..." Red splotches formed on his bald head and neck. "I repaid a great favor to your parents in issuing this proposal, but now I can see a woman like you has a heart unlikely to be touched. You will indeed become the next batty Lucinda Brinley."

Maisie felt slapped by the insult. No one had dared to call her out for her comments. The woman no man wants? When her mother said these words, they had far less punch. A heart unlikely to be touched? He even compared her to crazy Aunt Lucinda. Dinner turned in her stomach. The room swirled. The heavy furniture crowded the room.

He snapped shut his mouth. "I'm sorry. I have said too much. I will leave you, now."

Plucking at his mustache, Mr. Pope hushed his tone, perhaps because of Maisie's silence. Like a hot air balloon, Mr. Pope floated from the room.

Through the open door, Mother stared after Mr.

Pope with mouth agape in the foyer. Then she turned toward Maisie. Light burned in her eyes. And something else—her shoulders sagged—disappointment.

Maisie blinked away tears. The truth of Mr. Pope's words stung. Her mother's expression of horror ached her heart. She would never find a man worthy of the secret thoughts and affections of her heart. Couldn't she find a man whose heart yearned for warmth and companionship, but not a dowry? She would never find him—not among the Boston elite. Running past her mother, she rushed up stairs, tripping over the skirt hem in her haste. A loud rip sounded. She would end an old maid. And she didn't know how to stop it.

****

Outside, in the shade of his shop, Cyrus tightened the lugs on his iron lattice work, securing them into the brick. In the last three weeks since those rowdies threatened his shop, he'd completed iron bars to protect the windows. The cool morning breeze chilled him.

"Whatcha doing?" Even in the shadows, Captain Christopher Peele's Calvary uniform's buttons shone.

"Just finishing installing these iron bars." He examined them for any weakness. Grasping the metal scrolls, he shook them for good measure.

Christopher pointed to Cyrus's work. "Bars? Why they are too pretty to be called bars."

Cyrus stood back. True, he put in more effort than he should've creating them. His bars had more ornate scrollwork than the staircase at the White House. The local blacksmith probably could've done a faster job, but Cyrus wouldn't have any ugly parallel bars on his gunsmith shop. "You don't think they're too decorative, do you?" The vines trailed up and around each vertical bar. Perhaps he could've spent less time fashioning each grape and leaf. He bit his lip. Too late now.

Christopher grinned and slapped Cyrus's right shoulder. "No, they're perfect. Just what I'd expect from you. What are the bars for?"

"Added security measures." He hadn't told him or anyone about Gambell's gang. He hoped he'd seen the last of them.

Christopher tilted his head. "They are rather decorative."

Cyrus gathered his tools. "Come inside! Why the unexpected visit? What are you doing in town?" He led the captain inside to the cooler interior of his shop. He hadn't lit the forge yet, and the new bars prevented a measure of light coming in. He laid his tools on a bench.

"Well, to be honest. I'm tired of riding the range. I'm ready to settle down."

"You? Settle down?" Christopher wasn't known to have any steady girls. He only kept company with the Social Club girls when he came into town. Cyrus stroked the coal with a rake, gathering the gravel-sized coal coke into a center. He set his foot to pump the bellows, but then remembered he'd just purchased a new hand crank fan. He lit the forge and cranked the fan below to get the fire going. No, the foot pump worked better.

Captain Peele leaned against the wide brick chimney. He swept soot off his tan pants. "I've been thinking. I'm twenty-six. I need to start thinking of marriage and family."

Cyrus nodded. Although a good six years older

than the captain, he agreed but said nothing. His own prospect ran short back in his small Pennsylvania town. He guessed his chances of marrying out here, where the men outnumbered the women seven to one, were slim to none.

"You plan to head east to find a bride?" Cyrus focused on the glowing embers burning at the heart of his forge. He glanced up.

Christopher shook his head. "Can't leave my post."

Cyrus shook his head. "There aren't many women here—not many of the age and disposition to marry."

"True." He coughed. "I, uh, I've been writing a few young ladies."

Cyrus raised his eyebrows. "Have you?" He was surprised the captain could even write, let alone compose a whole epistle. "And how is letter-writing working for you?"

Captain Peele's face crumpled. "Terrible. That's why I came to talk to you. I've written to several different women who have all rejected me."

"How did you get introduced to these women?"

The captain shrugged. "The local pastor sends letters to other parishes around the country to women seeking to make a connection." His eyes lit up. "Scores of women are desperate to find a man."

Cyrus laughed inside. How opposite of Wylder. "So what seems to be the problem?"

Christopher covered his face with his hands. "I can't get any of them to write me back."

"How many have you sent?"

"About seventy." He dropped his hands.

Cyrus raised his eyebrows. "Oh dear."

Christopher leaned across the forge. "I have an

idea. You're a great writer. You have a way with words. Why don't you write the first letter? They'll think it's from me and write back."

"I can't do that." Cyrus moved past him to grab his file.

"Why not?"

"First off, it's deceptive. And second…" He couldn't imagine sending off a letter to a desperate woman and hoping she'd come out here for a promise of marriage. The whole thing sounded cheap. And desperate for all parties concerned. With his file, he sawed away on a rod.

"You can't come up with another reason. Helping me write a letter is not deceptive. You'd be coaching me—teaching me what to say and how to say it. I find it unfair to have the dashing good looks of a god but not have the ability to say the words that get girls to do things."

Cyrus stopped filing. He narrowed his eyes. "What sort of things?" He wasn't about to write letters of any illicit nature or persuade young women to lose their virtue.

Christopher opened his arms. "Marriage. I just want to find a girl who sees past my bad writing and will want to leave all she knows to marry me. Once she sees me, I know she won't regret her choice." He stuck his hands on his hips and jutted his chin upward.

Cyrus shook his head. Yes, many women in town fawned over Captain Peele. His dimpled cheeks, sunny hair, and his bright eyes made even married women smile and blush.

Raising his eyebrows, Christopher licked his lips. "I need help getting her here."

Arranging his hammer and file on his bench, Cyrus sighed. He couldn't leave his friend alone in a plight. Offering a few helpful words wouldn't be the end of the world. "All right. What have you written so far?"

Captain Peele grinned. He pulled a paper from his blue jacket. "Here." He cleared his throat. "'My name is Captain Christopher Peele. I am looking for a woman who will come to Wyoming and marry me. I like horses and polishing my boots. My good looks will please you.'" Christopher clutched the paper in both hands and raised his eyebrows. "What do you think?"

Cyrus fiddled with his wedge. He struggled to keep a laugh from belching out of his chest. He couldn't believe Christopher wrote something so daft. "Hm. I think you need to redraft it."

"The whole letter? It's not good, is it?"

Cyrus shook his head. "It just needs a second draft."

Lowering his hands, Christopher's shoulders slumped. "This is already my fifteenth draft."

Rubbing his temples, Cyrus raised his eyebrows. He inhaled. "Okay. Well. First off." He took the paper. "Don't talk about yourself. Ask her questions." Clearing the bench, he drew another parchment from a drawer and sat. Dipping his metal pen into the inkwell, he paused over the new piece of paper. "You don't know who you are writing?"

"Not at first. I give my letter to the pastor who sends them to other pastors across the US. Then if a woman is interested, she'll write back."

Cyrus ran a thumb across his lip. "Okay, so maybe you'll want to introduce yourself but also ask her about herself. You want her excited to write back." He bent over the paper and wrote.

"Yes." Captain Peele leaned over his shoulder. "And you have such nice handwriting, too."

Cyrus raised his head. "I just wrote the date. You should always date your letters."

Christopher clapped his hands. "All right. And then?"

"You need a greeting."

"'My lovely lady of my choice.' "

Cyrus shook his head. No doubt Christopher had heard that phrase somewhere. "No, you haven't met her. You need to compliment her sincerely yet subtly. You don't want her running away. You want her to be intrigued."

Christopher nodded. He raised his eyebrows. "Okay, so how do I do that?"

"Like this, 'My hopeful friend.' "

With peaked eyebrows, he widened his eyes. "Friend? I want us to be lovers."

"That will come in time, but first, she needs to be coaxed with gentle words. If you rush it, she'll run scared. Creating a friendship with a woman is like tempering metal. If you hurry a relationship, you'll create brittle material—something as easily shattered as glass. But if you take your time, you will find refined, strong, and useful metal."

"Okay. Then I want to go for the refined metal." He rubbed his hands along his trousers.

Cyrus frowned. He couldn't concentrate with Christopher's sweaty, horsey breathing over his shoulder while he wrote. "Why don't you leave this letter with me overnight? I'll compose something tonight, and you can pick it up in the morning."

Grinning from ear to ear, Christopher nodded. "Sounds good. Really good. Thank you so much. You're the best friend a man could have." He picked up his hat, slapped it on his head, tripped over the oak barrels, and thundered out the door.

Cyrus had never seen anyone so hopeful. He chewed on the end of the pen. Now what to write?

Chapter 3

The only reason Maisie's mother allowed Pastor Wilkinson in her home was because he completed his divinity degree at Harvard. The pastor must've been in his early fifties with a young, energetic body, a shock of dark hair that most certainly had a bit of shoe polish added, and a ready smile. He came over more often lately, and Maisie couldn't figure out why.

She dared not to ask Mother. Since the incident with Ralph Pope, her mother barely spoke to Maisie. Peace at last. Maisie was never more delighted.

After their usual dinner, Maisie sat in the sitting room near the fireplace bent over her needlework for recovering a chair she'd worked on inconsistently for years. Fire crackled under the mantel below the famous gun. Maisie's fingers deftly handled the needle in and out. In and out. Why was the pastor still here? Hadn't he a sermon to prepare? She yawned. He and her parents discussed...Oh, dear. She had no idea. She hadn't paid an ounce of attention. His silky voice always lulled her to sleep.

"...And that's when I returned from St. Louis." The pastor, clad all in black, leaned into the high-backed chair.

His statement caught Maisie's ears. "Have you really been out as far west as St. Louis? It must be the edge of the world." Maisie leaned forward in her overstuffed and uncomfortable chair, soaking in every detail. Finally the pastor said something worth paying attention to. "What is it like?" She dropped her half-finished needlepoint into her lap.

"St. Louis is a beautiful city set near a very large river—the Mississippi."

A youthful grin crossed his features. He ran a hand down his lean thighs clad in dark pants. He fiddled with the white ruff at his neck. Maisie nodded.

He spanned open his hands. "They say that the river in some places is a whole mile across."

Maisie raised her eyebrows. "I have read all about the adventures of James Orton exploring the Amazon Valley. Imagine, America has a river almost as big as the Amazon, and I have never seen it!" She sat back.

Mother scowled. "Boston has many beautiful tributaries. The Charles River is extraordinary. Why would you want to see anything else?"

Maisie sat forward again. "America has so much to offer. We see but a tiny portion here. Do you ever wish you could go live out West?"

Pastor Wilkinson glanced to Mother. "I believe we have everything we need right here in Boston."

"You are a diplomat, Pastor Wilkinson." Maisie resumed her needlepoint.

He shared a smile across the room.

"Our beloved pastor has come to talk to you about marriage, Margaret, dear." She turned to the pastor. "She has refused twelve men."

"Don't you believe in matrimony?" He raised a brow. "It is ordained by God."

Maisie straightened her spine. "It is not the institution I object to, rather the prospects."

Mother sighed.

Pastor Wilkinson shot her a glance. Then he smiled at Maisie. "Well, perhaps we can do something about the prospects."

Sweat pricked her armpits. Heat rushed to her face. Maisie arranged her skirts in a chair. "I am perfectly capable of finding my own husband."

Mother stood in front of the fireplace. "You haven't impressed me with the best judgment."

"You've embarrassed me inviting the pastor here. Now he'll think I'm incapable of finding my own match." She tossed him a tight smile.

Waving her handkerchief, Mother paced in front of the hearth. The rustle of her silk under-skirts drowned the sound of the fire crackling. "You've embarrassed me by jilting Harold Peabody. Such an old family and so connected. Everyone said you were such a perfect match."

Perfect match? She shuddered. "If you'll only let me explain—"

Mother waved her scented handkerchief. "I'm not interested in why you rejected such an eligible man."

Lavender floated around the room.

Two lines formed in the space between Mother's brows. More than a hint of impatience laced her words. Maisie fumed. Mother's refusal to listen hurt more than Harold's betrayal. Mother smiled as if she were not involved in an unpleasant conversation. Rolling her eyes, Maisie sat straighter.

Pastor Wilkinson coughed and crossed the room with a spry step. He stood near her.

"You are here to play matchmaker?" Maisie plucked threads from her skirts.

"Your parents did probe me about a few young men." He slid her a sly smile. "But I have something different in mind."

Intrigued, Maisie sat forward. The good pastor was on her side.

"Margaret, dear." Mother waved her handkerchief. "Why don't you play for the pastor? Margaret has been playing since she was a child and has the perfect lightness of touch."

A flame lit in Pastor Wilkinson's eyes.

"I'll turn the pages." He stood and held out his elbow.

"You are a true gentleman." She took his elbow. He escorted her to the piano in the center of the sitting room.

She adjusted the oil lamp above the piano. "What shall I play?" She nodded toward the box near the instrument. "You are welcome to look through the music." Arranging her skirts, she sat at the bench and played a piece from memory.

The pastor shuffled through sheet music and dropped one. He bent to pick it up. Papers slid from his inner breast pocket and landed on the thick, plush carpet.

"What are those?" She jutted her chin toward the papers.

"Oh, these?" He arched a brow. "Letters from men on the frontier searching for suitable brides. I have been commissioned to find low-born women willing to correspond and perhaps kindle a friendship into romance. The men have been recommended by other pastors throughout the nation. We would never send one of our precious lambs out into the wilds without proper protections. These men live in uncharted territory of the West. They need hardworking wives accustomed to daily labor." He set the letters on the piano near the music stand.

The letters called to her. Maisie reached for them.

"Music, Margaret," Mother called across the room.

Maisie placed her fingers on the piano again and began the ominous strains of Beethoven's *Fifth Symphony*. She eyed the letters. "Where might these men live?"

"Oh, all over. Illinois, Ohio, a few in Kansas, even the Wyoming Territory."

"Something more cheerful." Mother called again.

Immediately, she switched to Mendelssohn's *Overture to a Midsummer Night's Dream*. She swept the keys in rapid succession, yet she centered her focus on the letters. Such possibilities. "May I read one?"

Pastor Wilkinson raised his eyebrows.

Heat rose from her collar. "My maid is searching for a different life." The lie burned her chest and tongue. Lying to a pastor! She headed to the other place for sure.

"Margaret!" Mother cried. "Something not so modern. What an impression you'll give the pastor. Play the classics. Mozart, perhaps?"

She yanked her fingers from the keyboard then started on Mozart's *Sonata in C major*.

The pastor leaned closer. A light gleamed in his eye. "I'd be happy to leave them in your company. You may read them to her. Perhaps your maid will form a connection."

A lightness filtered through her. She sighed. Mother would never allow her to leave or marry an unknown man of unknown family clear in Timbuktu. Without her fingers leaving the keys, she smiled at Pastor Wilkinson. She finished her piece, embraced the stack of letters, and slid them in her pocket to read later. Such possibilities filled her. What did the letters contain?

****

When the door closed for the evening, Maisie, freed from her parents and even Pastor Wilkinson, bounded up the stairs, clutching her skirts.

In her room, Cara waited to help Maisie disrobe.

"I don't think I shall ever marry." Maisie sighed.

Earlier, Pastor Wilkinson droned on and on about eligible men along the eastern seaboard. Mother's eyes grew large. She gripped her hankie and twisted it. She always had such high expectations for Maisie.

Cara unlaced her spiral cording. "What makes ye say that, miss? Yer so beautiful—the envy of all the young ladies."

The sixteen-year-olds laughed at her behind her back. "As Ralph Pope said, my personality offends the men." She waited for Cara to reprove Mr. Pope and rush to Maisie's defense. "What do you think?"

Cara helped her out of her skirt and untied the bum pillow at her waist. "If I may speak freely…"

"You know you can."

"Yer always *slagging* the men who come to court ye, ye know."

Her Irish lilt made even a chiding sound like a song. "I don't understand your slang."

Cara crumpled her brow. "Men don't like to be made fun of. They want their woman to respect them."

Maisie's face flushed at her accusation. "Boston

35

men seem silly." Didn't anyone see how she improved? She hadn't spoken one uncivil word to the pastor about any of the men he suggested.

"Might it help if ye were a wee less particular?" Cara folded her dress and brushed it.

Papers slid from her pocket.

"What's this?" Cara bent and retrieved the letters.

"Oh, the letters!" Maisie snatched them. "I'd forgotten all about them!" The paper crinkled at her touch. She straightened the pile.

Cara furrowed her reddish-blonde eyebrows. "What are they?"

The color of her light green servant's uniform suited her pale skin. "Men searching for a bride."

Cara's face crumpled. "I canno' believe such a thing exists."

Maisie quickly raised the letters. "Don't worry. They've all been recommended by pastors so they aren't tyrants or drunkards. And they aren't stuffy men like those here in Boston, either. They are pioneer men—real men who earn their keep with their hands. The pastor gave them to me."

Cara narrowed her eyes. "Does yer mother know?"

"No! I told him they are for you!" A bead of excitement trilled in Maisie's chest.

Pink rose to Cara's cheeks. She swore upon the holy family.

"Shall we read them together?" Maisie jumped on her bed and tucked her feet beneath her. She adjusted the oil lamp on her bedside table to shed greater light.

Cara's green eyes sparkled. "Aye!" She laid the dress on a chair and sat on the bed with Maisie.

She unfolded the first letter. The handwriting was

big and scrawling, but he was a man so he was excused from the more genteel arts. "Here's one from Illinois. '*I live on a small farm. I expect a woman to help with the chores, the housework, and the laying up fruits for the winter and selling in town. If she knows how to drive a wagon, even better.*' This isn't a letter this is an advertisement." She shook her head and dropped it to the duvet. "Another one. '*Dear Miss—, I hope you are well. My name is Dershal Hines. I live in Kansas, as you see by my return address. My wife passed recently...*' Oh, a widower." How disappointing! She lowered the letter. "I don't know if I want a widower, do you? I think I'd rather start from scratch and not have to worry about competing with a wife who has passed. One never lives up to the expectations placed upon them by a first wife."

"Aye."

" '*...and I have six young children...*' "

"Six!" Again, Cara invoked the holy family.

Biting her lip, Maisie sighed. "Indeed. And his handwriting is awfully sloppy. One can always tell the character of a man by his hand." Maisie dropped the letter with the first. She retrieved another paper from the stack. "Here is one from Captain Christopher Peele." She turned to Cara and raised her eyebrows. "Sounds promising."

A grin pressed upon Cara's lips. "A captain, ye say? I like the sound of that." She wrapped her arm around Maisie's. "I like me a man in uniform."

"All those brass buttons." Maisie leaned closer so Cara could read the letter, too. "And such nice handwriting. Ahem! '*My hopeful friend, I am writing you from the wilds of Wyoming. I warn you, miss, if you* are not familiar with Wylder weather, the nights are cool here, yet the crucible of hope burns within me for the comfort of a little warmth.' " Sighing, she placed the letter against her chest. " 'The crucible of hope.' He hints at loneliness but only implies, not overtly states, his want for a companion. His words possess a hint of vulnerability without desperation." A connection struck her heart. At last, here was a man worth investing in.

"He expresses himself *quare* well."

A tremor of excitement trilled up Maisie's spine. She closed her eyes, imagining what Captain Peele must look like—dark, ruggedly handsome, streetwise, and handy with a gun. "I dare say he must be dashing."

"And tall."

"And rides well." Now her pretended Captain Peele rode a horse in a blue Calvary uniform.

"He must if he be an officer."

She opened her eyes. "I shall respond to this one." She leaped off the bed to the writing desk.

Cara leaned against the desk. "What shall ye say?"

At her desk, Maisie unfolded the letter and placed it next to her stack of stationery with a gilded, embossed MB on the letterhead. "He asks all sorts of questions here." She opened her inkwell. "I shall do my best to respond." With her pen poised above the inkwell, she paused. "What if he doesn't like me? What if some other woman has already snatched him up?"

"Don't worry, miss." Cara tossed her a grin. "Even though ye've shunned every man in Boston, America is still a big place. Besides, this letter was dated only a week ago." She winked. "I doubt he's fallen in love since then. I'm sure ye have time to woo him yet."

Buoyed by Cara's confidence, she dipped her pen

and began to write. He asked about her dreams: To do something heroic enough to be in a newspaper. Might he laugh at her silliness? Might he find her childish? Or worse, ambitious. She chewed on the end of the pen. Perhaps she should say she wanted to visit the place called Yellowstone to see the geyser that spurted hot water into the air at the exact same time every day. She went with the latter, deciding the former sounded too silly. She wanted him to like her. Her hands trembled as she wrote and hoped he did not see the squiggles in her lettering. Her mother would be ashamed of her sad composition, but yet, she wrote it in haste. Might this correspondence lead her to finally find true love?

Chapter 4

Clanking the hammer against the anvil in his shop, Cyrus worked away his memories of gunshots, screams, and cries of the battlefield.

"Somebody wrote back!" Christopher appeared next to him.

Cyrus must've been too absorbed in his thoughts to hear him come in. He needed to be more careful when he worked and not focus so hard, or someone would sneak up.

With a grin, Christopher held out a paper with gold-embossed letterhead. "I finally snagged one. A lady wrote me back! A Miss Maisie Brinley."

In a manner of speaking, she wrote Cyrus, but he wasn't one to spoil good humors. "What did she say?"

He grasped the paper between his two gloved hands. "She answered your questions. She's from upper-class Boston and is twenty-six."

"Congratulations." A prick in his heart caused a hint of bitterness to creep into his voice. Christopher enjoyed good luck where women were concerned. "You have your woman." She must've been as ugly as an old boot. If she was from old stock Boston with more money than sense. Likely, something was wrong with her not to be snatched up by all the bankers and merchants. "Now you can write her and persuade her to come out here to marry you."

Christopher's shoulders slumped as he dropped the paper. "I can't do that."

"Why not?" He stilled his hammer.

"I told you. I don't have the words. I need you to write it for me."

Cyrus placed a hand on his hips. "I can't write letters for you." He did the first one as a favor. He didn't have time for Christopher to dictate everything.

Waving the paper, Christopher clasped his hands together. "But you have to. If she read what I would write, she'd realize I'm a dunderhead and stop writing me."

"Maybe that's for the best." Cyrus faced the bench and strapped a length of steel into the vise to cut with a file.

"You have to help me."

Cyrus shook his head. "I helped you get a response. That's more than you've gotten before."

Christopher clasped his hands. "Please, just help me write letters until she's safely here in Wylder. I can't do it without you. I can't leave my post, and I'm stuck here until I get a command. Help me, please."

Cyrus screwed the collier in the vise. The desperation in Christopher's voice tore at his heart. "Let me see the letter."

With a wide smile, Christopher passed him the letter.

Cyrus unfolded it. She had an elegant hand. Her words flowed seamlessly. " '*I always desired to visit the hills of Wyoming Territory and see the great wonders of nature.*' " He smiled to himself. Most of the territory was flat, boring, and filled with nothing but sagebrush and cattle. Perhaps she'd be a bit disappointed. At the end, she asked Christopher a question. " '*What do you look like? I just want to know so I can be accurate in my imagination.*' " A hint of laughter gurgled from his throat. At least in his description of Christopher, he could be honest.

"Will you write her?"

Cyrus barely heard. He'd already taken out his pen and dipped it into the inkwell. He dated the letter.

" '*The wilds of Wyoming Territory are to be tamed by those who have the courage to take raw beauty and craft it into brilliance.*' " He spoke as the pen scratched across the rough paper. " '*If you have the fortitude and patience, you can learn to love it here. Our town is no refined Boston—no cobbled streets, no great architects, and no grand design. But the history here is for the making. Wyoming is for dreamers, creators, and visionaries; for its history will be our future.*' "

As to the part of his description, he smiled as he described Christopher. " '*I hate to say this but I am a towhead, cursed with hair the color of straw. My arms are barely strong enough to control my horse, but they will be strong enough to hold you, my dear, should you deem me worthy of a visit.*' "

When he turned to ask Christopher a question, Cyrus saw only an empty shop. Sometime during his writing, Christopher sneaked out.

Shrugging, Cyrus returned to his letter, trimming the lantern over his bench. He asked her other questions—about her life in Boston and her family. How could he tease out her appearance? A woman like her wasn't likely to come out openly and admit she had the skin of a hag. But what if she were as ugly as an old carpet bag? Would the handsome and winsome

Christopher reject her once she alighted from the train? He wagered Christopher would not likely marry a woman he thought unequal in looks. Asking her about what she thought about her appearance so soon sounded too shallow. He would only ask if she decided to come. If she came, then he could ask so that he might recognize her at the train depot.

At the end, he couldn't bear to write Christopher's name at the bottom of the epistle. He could not forge his name. A man's name was his sacred title. It belonged to him and only him. Forging a man's signature was akin to sleeping with his wife—underhanded and possibly illegal. No, he couldn't attribute these words to Christopher. In the end, he only signed with a simple cursive *C*.

****

Maisie checked the entry table for mail several times a day. At every knock at the door, she raced to the leaded glass door and threw it open, only to be disappointed to see the milkman with his newly patented glass bottles—everyone had a patent for everything these days—or one of the Fine Ladies who visited Mother or one of the members of the Watch and Warn Society soliciting donations for the cause of protecting human decency.

Slumping, she gave up and went upstairs to read the atlas on her bed. Perhaps Captain Peele was unimpressed with her letter or already wrote another more interesting woman—one even more well spoken and witty. The thought burned in her chest. She threw aside the atlas and picked up the Dickens novel. At least Dickens could distract her from her terrible thoughts.

A knock sounded on the door. Cara entered with a coy smile on her lips.

Maisie sat up.

"A letter's come for ye, miss."

Clapping her hands, Maisie threw down Dickens and jumped off the bed to grasp the letter. Her fingers shook unfolding the papers. "It is from him!" She didn't need to mention his name. She dreamed of his name, spoke it on her lips in her prayers, and carried it in her heart. Tucking her skirts beneath her, she curled up on her chaise near the window and tossed back the damask curtains for better light.

Cara sank next to her and brushed her linen apron.

Maisie passed her gaze eagerly over the sentences. How each word thrilled her. "Oh dear, he's blond." Her shoulders sagged.

"Does that discourage ye?" Cara sat back.

Maisie laid the letter in her lap. "I just don't find blonds attractive, that's all. And he's thin."

"He didn't say that." Cara tugged the paper closer and scanned the letter.

"He implied it."

"Ye don't have to write him."

Maisie sighed and picked up the letter again. His words were so beautiful and spoke to her soul. Were not the connections of hearts more valuable than the color of hair? "I've decided I don't care what he looks like."

Cara narrowed her eyes. "Are ye sure? What if he has the face of a gargoyle? Or has bad breath? Or a drinking habit? Or spits tobacco on the floor at dinner?"

Shrugging, Maisie inhaled. "I love his heart. As long as he is sensible, a hard worker, and someone of keen feeling, I will be happy."

Cara arched a brow.

Maisy snatched her hand. "Come now, let's not focus on appearances. Read this." The sentence about Wyoming thrilled her. She possessed this kind of grit. " *'The dreamers, the creators, the visionaries.'* I love it." She clasped it to her chest. "What should I write him next?"

****

Excerpts from letters between Maisie and Cyrus May and June of 1879:

You do not ask me, sir, about my looks.

I don't ask you because if you are as beautiful as your thoughts then you are Aphrodite herself.

Then looks aren't important to you?

You've detected me. I am blind to all but the most penetrating beauty. When you come to Wyoming Territory, I will be the judge myself. You do not need to aid me in drawing my own conclusions with descriptions which will no doubt be a self-deprecating estimation of your beauty.

Do you lie when you say you are weak?

I never lie, and I would never lie to you.

Then you jest about your strength.

Perhaps I teased you a little. You will have to come to Wyoming Territory to find out.

You are a terrible flirt, sir!

You are the first to accuse me of such behavior. You must bring this out in me and have changed my nature, or I am lowering my inhibitions around you. Either way, you are to blame for my recklessness.

Do you call yourself reckless, sir? You are not in

the habit of writing young ladies with the purpose of persuading her into marriage?

I am not in the habit of writing young ladies, period. You are the first, the only. I think I am falling in love with you, Maisie Brinley.

Chapter 5

One late June morning, Maisie woke with a kink in her neck. Sliding her hand under the pillow, she caressed the stack of papers, hidden from her mother's prying eyes. The ache in her neck was nothing compared to the song in her heart. She reread the last letter. Captain Peele's words were her last conscious thought before drifting off to sleep. She hugged it to her heart again. He loved her. The world sang. The sun shone brighter. Milk tasted sweeter.

Cara entered with a stack of pressed skirts. "Good mornin'."

"Good morning." Maisie sat and hugged her goose-down pillow to her chest. Her hair tumbled about her shoulders over her lacy white nightgown. What were his words about daybreak? " 'Anticipating your letters is like awaiting the dawn.' "

"Did ye say somethin', miss?"

"Nothing." She waved a hand.

"Yer mother awaits ye downstairs in the sitting room, first thing."

"Gladly."

Cara arched a brow and struck a hand on her hip. "Since when did ye do anythin' willingly for yer mother?"

Maisie removed her night dress and stood in her combinations, ready to be dressed. She smiled over her shoulder.

Cara placed her dress for the day over her dressing table chair. "Yer pleasin' mood wouldn't have to do with letters from a certain somebody, would it?"

"Maybe." She scrambled back to her bed, where Cara plumped pillows and tightened the bed linens. "His words, Cara, are nectar to my soul. Listen to this. 'I both anticipate your coming and dread it at the same time. I have grown fond of our letters and will miss them if you come. Perhaps if you are here, we can still communicate by letter, though, no doubt, you would grow tired of only words, as I have.' And again here. 'And what if I do not live up to your expectations? What if you are disappointed in the man you thought you knew? What then? How can I be a cad and desire you so near, yet fear the look of disdain in your eyes when you meet me? I will no longer pressure you to come to Wyoming Territory.' " She kissed the words.

Dragging Maisie by the hand, Cara settled her in front of the wardrobe. "Are ye goin' to Wyoming, then?" She placed the corset around Maisie and tightened the loops and tied the laces at the top.

With help, Maisie slid on her silk stockings and attached them to her lacy combinations. "I still haven't decided. Leaving would break my mother's heart. But when I read such letters, happiness brims my soul. I think of nothing other than these words. I read them and savor them as I would a fine meal. They are a part of me now. I have memorized passages. They are manna from heaven in a wilderness of loneliness."

Helping her into her crinoline, Cara rolled her eyes. "Ye are *quare* dramatic. Hurry, yer mother awaits. And ye know how impatient she is." She placed the corset cover over the boning. Then she tied on the bum cushion. With a groan, she hauled the heavy skirts over Maisie's head.

Maisie slid on her tailored, long-sleeved bodice.

After binding up the bodice, Cara swept up Maisie's hair and pinned it in place. "I love yer raven hair." She fetched the button-hook.

Maisie hiked up her skirts and laid her foot on the upholstered stool.

Cara hooked up her black kid leather boots.

Sighing, Maisie lifted the latest letter from off her dressing table and tucked it into her pocket. The words gave her courage to face whatever tedious request her mother would ask. She thundered downstairs, careful to take the last few delicately lest she risk a lecture from Mother on ladylike behavior. She opened the large wooden doors to the sitting room.

Mother stood next to the fireplace, knotting her handkerchief around her forefinger.

Something was wrong. A pit formed in her stomach.

Mother lowered her eyes, showing two distinct lines between her brows. "I have good news." Mother stretched out both her hands.

Slowly, Maisie crossed the room. Just as she reached the table in the center of the room, she noticed someone else's presence.

In the high-backed chair sat Pastor Wilkinson. His leg jittered, and he kept his gaze focused on his shoes. He leaned forward and clenched his jaw then fiddled with the white ruffle at his neck.

He looked guilty or nervous. Oh, no! A shock bolted through her. He'd told her about the letters.

"I have a surprise." Mother smiled.

A light dawned. Her mother's agitation was happiness not anger. Maisie gulped. She slid a hand into her pocket to touch the letter for comfort. Nothing scared her more.

"The pastor has a proposal."

Maisie sucked in air. "You mean he's found someone who wants to marry me?"

Pastor Wilkinson coughed.

"No, dear." Mother spread a smile across her face. "He's proposing marriage. And your father and I have accepted."

The carpet opened beneath her. Her lungs halted. All the air disappeared from the room. Pastor Wilkinson was her ally to get out of Boston. He couldn't possibly see her as a potential wife. "But he's so old." He was more than twice her age.

He coughed again behind her.

She closed her eyes. Heat rose from her collar. She forgot he was still in the room. She opened her eyes. "Forgive me." She turned. Her heart thundered against her chest with the pace of a galloping horse. How could he do this? Marrying him would ruin everything. What of the letters?

Rising to his feet, he focused his gaze on the carpet. "I'll excuse myself if you wish to discuss this privately." He all but ran from the room.

The two lines appeared between her eyebrows again. "Margaret, time is running out. You need to get on with your life. The pastor is a good match." She plucked at Maisie's dress. "He is not so old, and he is well-connected. I don't know why I hadn't thought of him before."

"I cannot marry him." Words from the letters pierced her. How could she be happy with a pastor when another man sent such penetrating letters? She swallowed. Maisie was not one for fainting spells, but for the first time in her life, she felt weak. The room spun. The cloying smell of her mother's scented handkerchief sickened her. She needed to escape.

Without another word, she backed from her mother and ran upstairs. Once in her room, she threw herself on the bed. A cascade of letters slid from her pillow. How could she find a way to get to Wylder in Wyoming Territory?

****

Without a word, Cyrus slid another letter, not a penny postcard, to Miss Brinley toward the postmaster. He hoped no one else noticed in the busy, small clapboard post office. He'd taken to writing her on his own between the letters Christopher received. Often, while working in his shop, an idea or a phrase would come to him, and he thought to share it with Miss Brinley. He paid the postage and stepped out into the street.

"Yooo-hooo!"

One of the girls from the social club caught him by the elbow. He forgot her name. He raised his hat.

She hugged his upper arm. "My! I think your arms are getting stronger from pounding metal all day. When will you come visit us?"

Cyrus didn't enjoy the arm squeeze and focused straight ahead, lest his gaze wander to where her blouse dipped a little too low for propriety. "I've got lots of work to do. The shop keeps me busy." Only one woman made his heart gallop like an unbroken horse.

"Cyrus!" Christopher jogged across the street. "Oh, hello there, Miss Ruby." He bowed and removed his hat to the lady. He held it to his chest.

She dropped Cyrus's arm like a hot-potato. He shook his head with a hidden grin.

Her eyes grew wide. A grin blossomed on her painted lips. She waved a fan in front of her face and clutched Christopher's arm.

Cyrus rolled his eyes. Why did Christopher need Miss Brinley? He could have any woman in Wylder— at least until he opened his mouth.

"How are you doing?"

Winking, she clung to Christopher's forearm as if she couldn't walk without his help. Sheesh! She was so obvious.

Squinting in the sun, Christopher grinned. "I'm fine. I just stepped in a pile of horse-mess, though." He lifted his boot to show her.

She dropped her smile. Her lip curled. "Ew!" She fanned herself with more flurry.

Cyrus rolled his eyes. How could Christopher be utterly clueless?

Christopher pointed toward her hand. "Could I borrow your fan for a second?"

"What for?" She arched a painted brow.

"It's the perfect tool to dig out some of this crap from my boot."

Miss Ruby dropped her grip, pouted her lips, and crumpled her brow. Then with a flip of her skirts, she turned on her heel and stalked away.

Cyrus stifled a chuckle.

"What did I say?" Christopher tossed up his hands. "I need to talk to you, anyhow."

Guilt burned in Cyrus's belly. Miss Brinley must've written him about something he wrote and sent without him knowing. He walked down the boards of Sidewinder Lane, keeping his focus straight ahead. Christopher smelled of horse plop and sweat. He must've just returned from his training exercises.

Resettling his hat on his head, Christopher gasped. "She's coming. She's coming here."

Cyrus didn't have to ask who. His stomach burned like a stoked fire. "Miss Brinley."

Christopher nodded.

Gulping, Cyrus inhaled to still his galloping heart. "When?" Miss Brinley was coming! His letters worked. He persuaded her to leave family and tradition to seek a better life here. But his heart sank. What did he do? Now that she was coming, he could no longer write her. Pain constricted his chest. And worse, if she came, she would marry the captain.

"By train next Tuesday." Christopher's eyes grew large. "What should I do? Once I open my mouth, she'll know I'm just a bumbling idiot."

At least Christopher was aware of his shortcomings. "Don't worry. She's not here yet. Did she agree to marry you?" Cyrus hadn't read her latest letter.

"She said she'd give us a week." Christopher kicked a dirt clod. "If she likes me, she's agreed to be married on Saturday, July fifth. A week!" He swept out his hands. "I don't know if I can keep up the pretense that long."

A thought gnawed in his mind like a file sawing metal. Cyrus didn't know if he could pretend he didn't love Miss Brinley that long.

****

Later that night, Cyrus worked in his shop. With each cut of his saw, he focused on Miss Brinley. Even as he worked in his shop, her letters captivated him. Yet, he was not the one who should be anticipating her coming. He both looked forward to and dreaded it at the same time. Of course, he could just avoid her. How often did a woman come into his shop? Not often. And he could avoid her for the week until she was safely Mrs. Christopher Peele. Ugh. His heart squeezed as if caught in a vise.

He checked his pocket watch. Nearly three a.m. Work helped him forget the outside world. He was married to his workbench and tools. Nobody else would have him. He finished a few repairs and polished them for tomorrow's pick up. Also, he slid a rope through the rifles and revolvers near the door on display and tied them to two metal loops on each end of the case.

With a bucket of slack tub water, he doused the forge. Smoke rose up the great brick chimney. Too late to walk home before opening the next morning, he settled in to sleep here for the night. After locking the doors, he trimmed his lantern.

With an old horse blanket, he nestled under his wooden work bench. Miss Brinley's words flashed in his mind. If only he knew what she looked like. He hugged the blanket around him. She had raven-black hair, was of average height and weight. Back during the war, he met men who carried huge black boxes and who replicated people on a plate. Cyrus wasn't sure how it was done, but he sure wished he had one of Miss Brinley. Her words themselves were coke to his fire.

The roof above him creaked.

Cyrus paused all but his heartbeat. Raising his head off the boards, he strained his ears to listen. Nothing. Must be some animals.

He laid back his head, his thoughts full of Miss Brinley. Moonlight poured in from the barred windows, illuminating his buckets and forge tools. He drifted off to blackened sleep.

Then someone appeared in front of him.

Cyrus barely caught a glimpse of the man with a handkerchief over his face, but his smell of unwashed flesh was familiar. Gambell kept his promise. He returned.

"Surprise, gunsmith."

Hot, reeking breath of beans, onions, and tooth decay blanketed him. A bright light flashed behind Cyrus's eyes. Pain radiated from his forehead. He groped for his gun at his side but couldn't find it. Warm liquid poured down his temple. This wasn't the first time that side of his face had been hit. Immediately, he was on the battlefield surrounded by gun smoke and hollers. Disoriented, he stood to face his attacker. His knees buckled underneath him. Then Gambell's chuckle sounded distant, and his shop faded to black.

Chapter 6

Gripping the duvet, Maisie pulled the covers over her clothes to hide her traveling dress. She lay in bed, staring toward the plaster cornices on her ceiling.

Mother turned down the gas piped through the walls for the lighting. "I hope you are not still angry with me. I am only doing what's best for you. Marriage to the pastor is a good match. Since you rejected all the suitors I presented, I have taken matters in my own hands. Someday, you'll grow to see the wisdom of my actions."

Maisie's wedding dress hung in her wardrobe ready for the wedding in two days. However, a wedding to the pastor would not take place. Instead of answering her mother, she rolled under her covers with her back to the door where Mother stood.

She sighed. "Good night, Margaret. We have much to do tomorrow."

Maisie waited until her mother retreated from the door, then swept off the covers. She grabbed a hook and buttoned up her shoes in the dark—not an easy feat. Snagging the wedding dress out of her wardrobe, she laid it on her bed. From under her table, she dragged her smallest trunk. She only had room for a few skirts, bodices, and maybe one hat.

The side door to the privy room creaked.

Maisie jumped. Her heart thundered. She raised a

hand to her heart. "Good heavens! You scared me!"

Cara's face poked through the darkness. "Ye canno' go alone. I'm comin' with ye."

Maisie bit her lip. Her heart swelled for her maid. For the last six nights, she and Cara had sewn as many greenbacks and coins as the bank allowed her to withdraw into the linings of her dresses. She clapped her hands on Cara's shoulders. "I cannot ask you to give up your life here. This is a good life, Cara. I don't know what Wyoming holds. I cannot promise you wages of a gentleman. I'll be a soldier's wife. You'll have to find your own work." If all went as planned, by this time next week, she'd be Mrs. Christopher Peele.

Nagging swelled in her heart. She shook it free. Freedom always cost a sacrifice of comfort.

Cara raised her reddish-blonde eyebrows. She swore upon the holy family. "Miss Maisie, I am comin' with ye."

"Stubborn Irish." Yet relief washed over her. Traveling alone was the part of the plan that scared her the most. Maisie folded skirts into her trunk. Christopher Peele sent money for her third-class ticket, but she exchanged it for first class. She could easily purchase another for Cara at the depot.

"Besides, ye wouldn't get very far without me." Winking, Cara gathered items from her room—the button hook, hat pins, silver-plated hair brush, and styling tools—with a slight smile. "Nothin' remains for me in Boston if ye leave. And ye are me closest friend."

Folding lacy combinations, an extra corset, stockings, and gloves, Maisie paused in her packing. "You've been my confidante through this whole ordeal. But if you come, you come as an equal. You'll not be calling me miss."

Cara bowed her head. "Yes, miss."

A sly twinkle blazed in her eye, even in the darkness. Maisie slapped her playfully with a corset before dropping it into the trunk.

"Are ye takin' yer dress?" She nodded to the heap of white silk on the bed.

Crepe flowers finished off the shoulders and held the drape in the front. All along the bottom, the flowers flowed as if they spilled from the shoulders. Maisie bit her lip. Mother ordered it from Paris weeks before even telling her of the proposal. The dress was the most beautiful thing she'd ever put against her skin. But it was sewn for a wedding to Pastor Wilkinson. "The dress will be the most ostentatious thing out in the wilds of Wyoming, don't you think?"

"No, that will be the woman wearin' it." Cara winked. "And I'm sure the captain won't mind."

"All right. Let's pack it." Warmth spread through her that Cara decided to come. But they had to hurry. The train left at midnight. She crumpled the dress and stuffed it on top. If nothing else she could sell it after the wedding. "Oh dear, but it won't fit in the trunk."

"We can put it in me carpet bag."

Cara left and returned with a thin cloak and a carpet bag.

Maisie stuffed the dress in the hideous-colored bag then wrapped a traveling cloak around her. She stood at the door of her room. An ache swelled in her heart. Crossing the Persian carpet, she made her bed, smelling the soap the servants used to clean the smooth linens. She returned the pillow. The letters slid from their hiding spot.

The letters! She almost forgot them. Wrapping them in a loose ribbon, she placed them in the bag along with her dress. She paced. Perhaps she should leave her mother a note. At the writing desk, she inked a pen and stared at the white paper. What to say?

Dear Mother,

I am leaving to start my own adventure. Do not worry for me. I will write more details when I am settled.

Perhaps Mother would forgive her once she wrote to say she was married. She signed and blotted the letter, folded it, and left it on the desk for her mother to find in the morning.

With Cara's help, Maisie hauled the trunk down the carpeted stairs. Once at the bottom, she noticed a light illuminated the hall. She whirled, fully expecting her mother to be in her night dress in the vestibule.

Instead, Grandpa Shaw stood in his smoking jacket holding a hurricane lamp.

The smell of tobacco rose to her nose. Memories flooded her mind.

He removed the pipe from his lips. "Where are you going?"

She expected the cabby at the front door any minute. She glanced at the light seeping in from the leaded glass. If Grandpa snitched, she'd never be free. "I'm running away for real this time."

Placing the clay pipe in his mouth, Grandpa smiled. "Good! Where are you going?"

Maisie slapped her gloves together. Was a lie better than the truth? She inhaled. She was too tired for falsehoods tonight. "Wyoming Territory."

He lifted his fuzzy white eyebrows, then he

narrowed his eyes and pointed with the pipe. "You'll need a gun."

She started. "I don't have one."

Tilting his head, Grandpa turned and headed for the sitting room.

Maisie followed, hoping to please him enough he wouldn't tattle to Mother.

He stood at the unlit fireplace. "Take the Brown Bess. She's been out of action too long. She hasn't been living up to her potential." His lamp illuminated the flintlock over the mantel. "Go ahead. It was always yours."

She plucked up the gun. It had an awkward weight—about ten pounds. But the muzzle-loader was longer than it looked on the wall. "How do I use it?"

Grandpa lifted the powder horn and purse from the mantel. "Powder goes in the flash pan. Stuff the ball and some wadding in the barrel with this." He tapped the ramrod with his forefinger. "Most likely you won't have to use it, but better to be prepared than caught unaware."

She tossed the purse with the metal balls over her shoulder, then strapped the powder horn over the other. She bent and kissed his rough cheek. The smell of tobacco overwhelmed her. Tears pricked her eyes. "I might never see you again."

Grandpa's eyes leaked moisture. "Oh, hush. Just take care of that gun. Lafayette gave it to my grandfather—"

"Yes, I know, I know." She shouldered the gun as if going off to war.

Cara appeared in the doorway. "The cabby's here."

"I have to go." She embraced him one more time

and imprinted the smell of his tobacco upon her memory forever. "I love you, Grandpa."

He clasped her elbow. "I'm proud of you, honey. You go, and write your own future."

With the flintlock over her shoulder, Maisie marched out the door and closed the chapter on her life as a Boston elite. As she stepped into the hansom cab, she felt her stomach turn. Would she survive the wilds of Wyoming?

****

Two days later, the train slowed. Maisie opened her aching eyes. Out the window, a platform rose. A sign for Clarksburg, Tennessee, flashed by. Due to repair work on a more northern line, they had to take a southern route.

Across from her on the unfolded bed in their private train car, Cara offered a dry crust of bread she pinched from the kitchen. "We're stoppin'."

"Thank you." Maisie stuffed the bite into her mouth. "I see." She stretched her arms around a lumpy pillow that felt like it had been stuffed with pickles rather than feathers. Bess lay beside her.

The wood paneling shone in the morning sun entering through a small carriage door set into the wall. Someone turned off the small lamps while they slept. Along the opposite side, a hallway connected their car with the other cars and led to the privy car.

She'd been two days on the road. Maisie had no idea Wyoming was so far away. She'd socialized with other passengers in the first-class cabin with velvet upholstered couches, heavy curtains, and wood tables.

When approached in conversation, Cara quickly lowered her head and cowered to the other fine ladies and gentlemen traveling in style. In their private car, Cara stretched out on one side of the bed.

Maisie slept on the other. Her back ached, and her dry eyes hurt. Already she missed her goose-down pillows and four-poster bed. She inhaled the smoky air coming in from the open window. "Why is this trip taking so long?"

The train slowed to a stop.

A steward would help restore the bed to seats soon.

Cara yawned and rolled over. "I heard in the first class car that the northern rail line needed repairs. We took an alternate route."

"This more southern route cost us an extra day." Maisie bit her lip. "I noticed you were uncomfortable in the first-class car."

"I'm not an equal, miss." Cara buried her head into her sleeve.

Maisie thrust up her chin. "Yes, you are! If you are to be an equal, you must see yourself as an equal."

Cara removed her arm. "What do ye mean, miss?"

Maisie furrowed her brow. How could she fit years of Mother's nagging into one conversation? "First off, no more lowering your head or your gaze when someone addresses you."

"But they can see I don't belong here."

Maisie reached across to lift Cara's chin. "We are no longer in Boston. This is the great West. It's a meritocracy. Classes no longer divide us. Those who prosper, do so on their wit, their grit, and their will to survive." A tentative smile grew on Cara's face. Maisie's words found their mark. "You've got plenty of all three, so I expect you'll make a fine frontierswoman. Far better than me."

Now her smile beamed.

Maisie raised her own chin. "So, stiffen your neck and don't let anyone say you are beneath them. You look them straight in the eye and you say, 'I have as much right as you to be here.' "

"Ye are so good, Miss Maisie. I'll not flinch again."

With warm satisfaction, Maisie settled back into the bench seating. Her future was brighter than her past.

At last, the train was on the move again. Time passed slowly, and Maisie drifted asleep to the lulling sway of the car. On the third day, Maisie peered out the window. Coming in to St. Louis, the train crossed a trestle bridge above a wide river. She pressed her nose against the glass. "Look, Cara! The American Amazon!" The brown water flowed below them, wider than any river she'd seen in Massachusetts. Thrills pierced her. She was living an adventure. At last, she'd seen the great river in America.

In St. Louis, a porter lugged her trunk to the next train.

She waited for a train switching. "I wonder what Grandpa is doing today." Had her mother forgiven her? Had she read the letter? Her mother would worry until Maisie wrote from Wyoming.

The damp air clung to her clothes. The heat was immeasurable. Could that big river really give off so much humidity?

Cara's red hair curled into ringlets at the base of her neck.

Soon, rain drizzled while Maisie waited. The view of the thick wooded trees and long prairie grasses thrilled her. What a change from the hustle and bustle of the city. She bought another loaf of bread and a small wheel of cheese from a vendor outside the train depot.

At last, the train left the damp and wooded lands of Missouri and chugged on toward Nebraska. Nebraska held little interest. Miles and miles of nothing but vibrant green prairie grass. Maisie tried to read, but the rocking of the train made it impossible not to get sick. Nausea bubbled up in her stomach. Her head ached.

Cara jumped up and opened the glass. "Yer face is turnin' green, miss."

Fresh air poured over her face. She held her chin aloft against the smell of it—grass and open air that reached both horizons. At least Missouri had trees. Maisie had never seen both horizons at once before. The golden sunsets took forever to hide behind a flat horizon.

"What is that huge black beast? Is it a bear?" Cara pointed out a window.

Herds of huge black beasts grazed across the grass. "Bison. I read about them in a book once." At least the animals offered some variety.

Cara dropped her jaw and stared. "What a creature!"

Small deer-like animals with long antlers jumped along the tracks. Their agility tickled Maisie. "Almost there."

Cara rose and smoothed her skirts. "I'll visit the privy, just to stretch my legs. I'm used to bein' on my feet all day. I canno' take all this sittin' around." She closed the glass door behind her. Then she quickly returned.

Cara's eyes were the size of saucers. Maisie's heart leaped in her chest.

"The train is bein' robbed."

Maisie bolted upright. "Robbed?"

"I peeked into the first-class car. Men, with coverin's over their faces, pointed guns at passengers. It's a robbery."

Maisie jumped to her feet. "Don't worry, Cara. They won't hurt you. I won't let them." Nerves shook Maisie. "Bess. Where's Bess?" To sleep, she'd laid the gun above on the luggage rack. With trembling hands, she loaded the gun, tearing off a piece of silk from the dust ruffle under her skirt for the wad. She jammed the rod down the barrel. She bit off the cork from the powder horn.

Screams echoed in cars down the hall.

Men shouted.

A gunshot sounded.

Gasping, Maisie dropped Bess. Exhaling with shaking breath, she retrieved the gun. How much powder should she put in the flash pan? She shook out a spoonful. Then she poured more. Better to have too much than too little.

A tall man with yellow hair opened their carriage door. A red bandana hid his face.

"Step back, and close the door." Maisie raised the musket. She had no idea how to hold the thing, but she prayed the determination in her voice and her brashness would scare him away.

"We don't want no trouble. Just turn over your valuables." Batting away the tip of her muzzle-loader, he waved a gun. "You don't know what you're doing."

Maisie swallowed hard. He was right, but she didn't want him to know it. He handled a gun better than she did, for sure. She raised Bess again. "Stand back, sir, or I'll shoot." She squinted her eye like she'd seen Grandfather do when he pretended to shoot and stared at the robber down the barrel of the gun. But her hands trembled. She couldn't keep the heavy thing steady.

"Go ahead." He lunged for the carpet bag. Creaking it open, he rifled through the contents. In one swift move, the robber snatched up the white silk wedding dress and tucked it into the crook of his arm.

A cloud of letters filled the air. The crosswinds between the open door and the window swirled them around the room.

"Not my letters!" The words she'd grown to love fluttered out the window. Others scuttled out the door. Her heart exploded. Faltering, Maisie dropped the gun to grab at the flying papers.

The wide end of the musket landed on the floor, pointing the barrel at a forty-five-degree angle toward the man.

A deafening sound rang through her ears. Smoke blurred her vision.

"You crazy woman! You shot me!" The man rocked back and dropped his gun onto the cabin floor. Swearing, he tore off his bandana from his face. Grimacing, he stuffed the bandana onto the blood blossoming on his upper left arm. His teeth were as yellow as his hair. And he was missing a few. The man spun and bolted out the door.

Smoke hung in the air with the pungent whiff of sulfur. Maisie stood in a stupor. She dropped to the seat. Most of her letters blew out the window.

"We traded a weddin' dress for a gun." Cara picked up the few remaining letters and the beautiful six-shooter with a carved handle the robber dropped. With wide eyes and open mouth, she closed the window. "I canno' believe ye shot him."

Maisie hung her head. "I didn't shoot him. The gun shot him." Chaos sounded around her—women continued to scream, gunshots fired, men shouted. A deep ache welled inside for the two stolen possessions, the dress and her letters. Both were irreplaceable.

The gun smoked at her feet. The Brown Bess had blown something fierce. The metal piece on top was completely shattered. What a disaster coming west had been! What made her think she knew anything about shooting a gun? She was not prepared for this kind of life. Had she made the wrong decision?

Chapter 7

After an hour stop in Cheyenne to change trains and to report the robbery to the officials, Maisie rolled into Wylder. Still heartsore from the loss of the letters, she hadn't spoken nearly the rest of the trip. Her ears still rang from the shot that broke the gun, and her head ached. With tangled hair and an aching body, she stepped from the train.

The porter helped her with the trunk, settling it onto the large shaded platform.

Maisie squinted into the sun. Across the dusty road from the shaded wooden train depot loomed the Five Star Saloon. It must not have gotten its name from the company kept there. Several men in dingy clothes hung outside the doors on the boardwalk.

They stared at Maisie and Cara.

Maisie avoided eye contact. Next door, the green-painted Rail Office stood next to the tracks and to the left, the Wells Fargo Stage Office loomed in the sun. Across the street to the right hung signs for the Supply Company, the barber, and the gunsmith's. Holding her hat against the wind, she peeked straight down Sidewinder Lane. A restaurant, theater, and a two-story dress shop lay beyond. The roofs of several other establishments clustered on the horizon. Clapboard houses, dirt roads, and dust were all she saw. She frowned. This town offered different scenery than the stately buildings in Boston.

"This is it?" She held a hand over her mouth. Her hand still reeked of sulfur. She bit her lip. "It's such a small town." She knew the town would be small from Christopher's letters, but seeing it in person brought the reality crashing down. Could she live here the rest of her life?

Cara stood next to her. She raised an eyebrow. "Looks about right. Remember, Cheyenne is only a train ride away."

Maisie held her breath. Where was Captain Peele? He was supposed to meet them at the platform. She wired him from Cheyenne. "You stay here. I'll walk around town and see if I can talk to someone about finding Captain Peele." A big, black powder burn still stained her dress. Her hair hung in uneven tendrils, judging by what she caught in the glass of the train. What a terrible first impression she'd give Captain Peele.

Across the platform, two unshaven men stared at Maisie. Guns swung around their waists. The wind carried their stench of body odor and liquor. Gulping, Maisie lifted her head high. She didn't appreciate their salacious grins.

"Take the gun." Cara slid the beautiful six-shooter into her hand. "Ye'll never know who ye might meet in this forsaken place." She cast a glance over the town. Her eyebrows peaked.

Maisie returned the gun. "You'll need it for your own protection. I'll take Brown Bess."

Cara nodded toward the gun. "That thing is no good now." She tsked and lowered her voice. "Yer grandfather would be so disappointed to see ye've busted the gun Lafayette gave to his granddad."

Maisie held up the flintlock. This gun had been in her family for generations. Her heart ached at the ruin. "Surely a smith can fix it."

"Ask him." Cara pointed across the street. "His shop's right over there. Can't hurt."

"Will you be safe here by yourself?" The sun never blazed like this in Boston. She blinked against the hot orb hovering a few handspans above the horizon. And even the air felt dry against her skin.

"I'll be fine." She raised her chin.

The two men in dingy clothes standing near the train master's office continued to stare and stroke their beards.

"Are you sure you don't want the gun?" Maisie held out the decorative one.

"Take 'em both. Ye're far prettier than me. Even dressed as ye are, everyone can see ye are a lady." Cara leaned in, eying the men. "And ye've got all the coin sewn into your linin'. Best take them." She leaned back. "And besides," she spoke louder. "I've learned to box with me brothers. If any man were to threaten me, I'd give them a reason to pay the doctor." She lifted her chin with a hint of a smile.

The men turned their backs.

Satisfied, Maisie left the platform with Brown Bess in one hand and the pretty six-shooter in the other. The dirt road reminded her this was new territory. She wasn't in Boston anymore. Shaking her head, she stepped into the dirt, heading for the store. Across the street, a gunsmith's shop sat near the Supply Store.

The sign hanging from a wrought iron arm read *Gunsmith*. Maisie headed for the door in the wooden structure.

"Hello there!" someone called.

She checked over her shoulder and up the street. She didn't see anyone. Where was the voice coming from?

"It's locked."

She looked up. Now she located the voice.

A man stood on the roof near the chimney, his form backlit by the sun.

Maisie tented her hand across her face. Against the sun, she couldn't see his face but only the outline of his athletic frame. His large, strong shoulders carried his head well. His legs stood sturdy on the split-wood shingled roof. With the grace of a man who worked his muscles, he spread a large metal mesh across the mouth of the chimney. Guns hung from his sides in a leather holster. "Are you the smith?"

He nodded. "I'm the gunsmith, yes. If you need a harrow fashioned, though, the blacksmith's up the road." With a type of hammer, he pointed toward town.

Maisie had no idea what he was talking about.

With a forearm, he wiped his brow. "But dressed like that, I'd guess you are no farmer."

The clanking of metal on metal sounded above her. Grinning, she shook her head. Men here weren't as threatening as she imagined. "No, not a farmer." Maisie surveyed the silk traveling dress she'd worn for nearly a week. But what could one expect when one travels? She frowned again at the black powder stain. Just from the walk from the train station to the smith's, her skirts were covered in dust. And her boots—she'd never had dirt in those buttonholes before. Thankfully, Captain Peele hadn't picked her up at the station. Before she met him, she needed a bath, a bed, and a fresh dress.

"You're no social club girl, either." More hitting sounded.

Moving, she cupped her hand over her eyes again to shield the sun for a better look. The smith intrigued her. "What do you mean social club?"

He chuckled low and soothing, like the rumbling of rain. Maisie blushed with realization. *A house of ill repute*. Her mother had warned her about places like that. She guarded against them in the Watch and Warn Society. Maisie doubted they had the old "W&W," as she called it, here in Wyoming Territory.

Pointing with his hammer, he paused. "You look like a woman of class and distinction, and I cannot figure out why you would be wandering the streets of Wylder."

The timbre of his voice thrilled her. She couldn't tell if he was teasing or being serious. Something about his friendliness tugged at her heart. A bead of happiness burst through her. But she was meant for Christopher. Nevertheless, a smile stole across her lips. "I'm actually looking for Captain Peele. Do you know him?" The hammer must've dropped from the smith's hands and landed on the roof with a thud.

He bent to pick it up. He held his hammer still for a few heartbeats while he stood on the roof facing her. "Yeah, I know him. What about him?" Clanking again.

She wasn't about to confess anything while yelling in the street. "Whatever are you doing up there?"

The clanking stopped. "Trying to burgle-proof my roof. A man sneaked down my chimney. That will never happen again."

Shaking her head, she couldn't understand the

context for his statement. "I need a gunsmith to fix this gun." She gulped at the wreckage. "It's a family heirloom."

He stopped hitting things. "Hold on. I'll be right down."

Maisie waited with bated breath. What did the gunsmith look like? And would he have the ability and knowledge to fix her cherished Revolutionary relic?

****

"Can you replace me teeth?" Gambell leaned back in a rickety chair at the dentist's office in Cheyenne. The chair groaned under his weight.

The dentist nodded.

Across the room, Douglas leaned against the apothecary's cabinet with probably a hundred drawers with little knobs.

He stroked his red beard. "We got other things to think about than your teeth."

"I have the money. I'm getting them replaced." Gambell nodded to the dentist seated next to him.

The scrawny dentist gave Gambell a side-eye glance. He held open a box. "With a nice selection of teeth, I think we can find something to stick in there." His teeth whistled as he spoke.

Gambell lifted his chin. "Where did you get those teeth?" The box reeked of cedar.

The dentist, shaking, picked up one and held it for the two to see. "They come from all over really. Some people sell their teeth. Some come from convicts. Others are from the dead."

Douglas slapped Gambell's shoulder. "You don't want no dead man's teeth in you. It's bad luck."

"I want these teeth replaced. Now that we've come

into some money…" Gambell swept back his hair and opened his mouth. "Fill me in."

"I'll just have to find similar sizes." The dentist peered in his mouth with a large magnifying glass attached to his head. "Oh my, you've got little teeth in here, don't you? Wait a moment. Let me see what's in the storeroom." He stifled a laugh with a trembling hand. "I'll be right back. We want them to fit as best we can." The dentist slipped out a back door of the office.

Douglas paced the wood floors. "We got to get out of here. We got the money we need to clear our desertion charges, now let's go. Every sheriff's office between here and Laramie will be looking for us. We gotta head south to Colorado to wire the money." Pausing, he stroked his beard. "You said that girl got a look at your face?"

Gambell nodded, rubbing the scruff on his chin. "She shot my left shoulder, too." As he did, he passed a hand over the burned hole on his jacket. He winced. The whole shoulder ached at night, keeping him awake. Only getting skunk drunk allowed him to sleep. "And she took my gun. I want her to pay."

Douglas shifted his head back and forth. His red hair swung around his neck. "We don't know who or where she is."

"I do." Gambell raised his eyebrows in succession.

"How would you know a thing like that?" Douglas's spurs whirled and clanked into the wood floors of the dentist office.

Gambell removed a few letters from the pocket of his coat. He found the letters among the pretty white dress when they camped for the night to count their spoils. "This letter is addressed to Maisie Brinley.

Apparently she's moving to Wylder to get married to some poor sap." Douglas took the letters and looked over them, even though he couldn't read.

"Back to Wylder?"

"Kill two birds with one stone." Gambell nodded. "I figure she owes me a new shoulder and a new gun, and the gunsmith owes me a new smile—at least some new teeth. Didn't the dentist say he can take them off dead people?" He let out a chuckle from deep within his chest.

Nodding, Douglas grinned. "Why didn't we just kill him when we took the guns?"

"Because he spared my life when he should've shot me after the war. A life for a life. Now he can pay. But that girl…" Gambell leaned back in the chair. "She saw my face. We can't let her live. She's one of the few people who could identify us."

Douglas's smile faltered. "So we have to kill her, too?" he whispered hoarsely.

The dentist opened the door. "These will work, Mr. Gambell, though they aren't exactly the right size. Seems like men with bigger teeth are more likely to sell than not. However, I've applied the proper adhesive. If you'll take another swig of the whiskey, lean back, and say *aah*, I'll apply them." He grinned with perfect white teeth all the same size.

With his good arm, Gambell grabbed the bottle next to his chair, took a swig, and leaned back. He would get those two, if it was the last thing he did.

****

Maisie stood in the shadow of the gunsmith shop out of the blaring sun, inspecting her muzzleloader.

The smith came round the corner of the building.

"What's wrong with your gun?"

She dropped her jaw. The man's face looked like it had been dragged along the streets. Fresh bruises swelled on his cheek. Underneath was old scar tissue. Maisie once saw a man who got his foot stuck in the stirrup while riding, and the horse pulled him for several feet along Beacon Hill. His face looked like raw meat. Had the same thing happened to this man? Angry pink scars criss-crossed the right side of his face. The shape of his right eye had been altered to be less round than the other. Shivering, she couldn't help but see only the unnatural skin and stepped back.

The smith never wavered in his gaze. His dark, serious eyes glared below a firm brow.

He thrust out his chin as if daring her to say something. Maisie inhaled.

Brushing back his dark hair, he stamped his foot.

After a few moments, she blushed. She finally tore away her gaze. Their encounter had been so pleasant until now. She focused on the musket. "I don't know what happened. I loaded the flash pan with powder...It dropped and, well, shot a man. It's kind of a long story." She fully expected him to cut her off as men often did.

But he only stared. "Go on. I'm happy to listen to long stories."

Tucking away a stray piece of hair, she handed him the flintlock. "Someone attacked me, and as I only had this for defense...I didn't know how much powder to use. I dropped it, and it exploded."

He took the piece and examined it, then focused his gaze on her.

The side of his face not marred by scars had nice

cheekbones and dark stubble along his defined jaw. A shock of straight, coal-black hair blew in the breeze. His eyes were kind, despite the misshapen one that drooped just a hair.

He leaned forward. "I'm sorry, did you say attack?"

"By train robbers."

He whistled low. "And you shot at him with this?" He held up Brown Bess and turned it in his hands.

"Yes." He held the gun with much more confidence than she did. "Accidentally, though. I don't know how to shoot."

"We'll have to change that."

A smile parted his scarred lips. For some reason, her heartbeat kicked up to a canter. "Somewhere on the plains, these robbers boarded the train. One came at us and stole…" A lump formed in her throat. All those letters flying through the window made her heart sick. "He stole several precious things. And he dropped this." She balanced the beautiful six-shooter on her open palm.

His eyebrows rose. "He had this gun?" Shouldering the musket, he took the handsome one.

"Yes. It's such a beautiful piece. I'm sorry to see it in the hands of a ruffian."

He lowered his eyebrows.

Over a pair of broad shoulders, he wore a loose, white poet's shirt, open at the front, exposing his collar bones. Coal or ash stains dotted the sides. A pair of suspenders pinned his flowing shirt to his body. He handled the gun expertly, as if it were an extension of his hand.

"It's one of mine."

"You sell to train robbers?" She grasped her throat.

He huffed. "No, they broke in here and stole several. Hence, the bars and now the grate over the chimney."

He nodded with his chin in the direction of the most ornately barred windows she'd ever seen and then toward the roof. Maisie gulped. Were bars so necessary out here? What kind of a town was Wylder?

He inspected the barrel. "Glad to have it back. You don't mind if I keep this do you? It is stolen property."

She held up her hand. "Please. I'm afraid I'm a little unprepared to shoot a gun." The image of the flash of light and the power of the gunpowder in her hands scarred her memory.

He nodded. "I'll make you a new one. One that will fit your hands better and will be small enough to hide on your person."

With the mention of her body, she flushed again. His gaze skittered over her. She wished the black powder had not marred her dress.

"And since I can't leave you defenseless, I'll give you a loaner until I'm finished with the new one."

She fanned her blazing face with a hanky. "You don't have to."

"But it's the right thing to do." He dipped his chin and squinted his dark eyes. "This is wild country out here. I'm glad you're safe."

Her insides burned like embers. "I was so sure the man would've killed us if the gun hadn't gone off. He was an evil specimen, with missing teeth."

He lowered his eyebrows. "Gambell. Did you report him?"

She nodded. "I told the stationmaster in Cheyenne.

They drew up a sketch that looked nothing like him." She tried to give the artist a better description, but he didn't listen.

"If it was the same band who stole my guns, we might identify these men. Sometime after you're settled, we can go to the sheriff's office. They can wire more information to Cheyenne. If they locate the men, they might recover your stolen property."

Maisie nodded. A light of hope for the recovered dress rekindled. But her heart still ached. They'd never recover the letters. His smile warmed her. Yes, despite the scar he was attractive. What was she thinking? She intended to marry Christopher Peele. "Yes, that would be good."

"Great." He hefted the muzzleloader from his shoulder and inspected it from the tip of the barrel to the butt. "The musket—it's a family heirloom?"

He arched his good brow. The other seemed held in place by scar tissue. She puffed out her chest. "Lafayette gave it to my great-great-grandfather in the Revolutionary War. So, do be careful with it." A flush rushed to her face. Must be the heat.

He shook his head. "This is no French gun."

"What?" She straightened her spine. Was he questioning her grandfather's story? She readied some careful remarks on his education.

"You see this mark? Every maker uses a unique mark to identify who made it, like a signature on a painting." He turned around the gun.

She could see the back end. Metal—brass maybe—covered the butt where she tucked it into her shoulder.

"Read this." His finger pointed to a small imprint in the metal.

She squinted to read the faint letters. "US." Heat tinged her cheeks.

"American made—probably in Pennsylvania." A grin splayed across his lips.

Maisie dropped her jaw. All those years her grandfather said Lafayette gave his grandfather this gun. Where did the story start? Was there another gun in the family? Maisie's head swirled.

He inspected the end, keeping the barrel pointed to the ground. "Come inside. Let's talk shop. My name's Cyrus Haddock." He stretched his hand.

"Maisie Brinley." She hesitated. Oh dear! She'd left her gloves at the station. Mother would be mortified. She took his hand. The texture of his hand was rough, and he had a firm grip. For some reason, he grinned. A pulse of lightning flashed through her fingers. She immediately dropped his hand. "Nice to meet you, Mr. Haddock."

Inside the shop the temperature dropped in the shade. A glow of coal lit a small fire under the large chimney. A cluttered workbench sat under a beautifully, yet maybe a tad intricate, barred window. A waist-high counter separated the shop from his workspace. Along the front two walls were vertical rows of guns in wooden boxes with a few empty spaces missing.

"Did you make all these?" Through the triggers ran a small chain, looped around and locked at each end into the wood display box.

Shrugging, Cyrus pumped bellows to grow the flame in his hearth. "Yes."

She ran a finger across the smooth barrels of the guns. Each handle was unique. "They're not just guns.

They're works of art." She turned again to admire their beauty.

"Thank you." Removing his gun belt, he hung an apron around his neck and tied it behind his back. "The commission pieces are hand-crafted. They can take three weeks to a month to make from scratch. The rest I create from pre-engineered standardized and tooled steel. Those guns are not so much work. I piece them together like a puzzle."

She admired the hand-made guns. Several uniquely carved and ornamental grips with hunting scenes stood out. "But they're still all beautiful."

"You flatter me." With a slight grin, he laid the musket on his bench. "Looks like you shattered the hammer when you set it off. How much powder did you put in there?"

Shrugging, she crossed to the counter. "Is there a set amount?"

Cyrus laughed. "Too much powder can explode the whole action. You're supposed to use as much powder as a lady *should* add sugar to her tea—about one teaspoon."

With a slight start, Maisie blushed. In Boston, she often added scoops of sugar behind her mother's back to sweeten her tea. She confessed that little detail once to describe herself to Christopher Peele. Did he know or just guessed her habits?

He held up the gun and squinted an eye. "I'm surprised the powder even still worked. Must've been kept dry."

"We kept the horn over the fireplace. Will that gun take long to fix?"

He ran a hand down the metal barrel. "Depends. I

can try to cast one here, or I can see if anyone already has a hammer made back East. Either way, I'll need time to repair it—possibly a week. These old guns are kinda tricky." He glanced up. "You don't mind leaving it here, do you?"

"Not at all." She had no use for a broken gun.

"But I can't leave you defenseless." He paced his shop. "You'll need a gun to protect yourself."

She opened her mouth to object. She was still a little traumatized from her last encounter with the muzzleloader.

He held up his hand. "I insist. No charge. Consider it a trade for bringing back the stolen piece. I'll deliver it as soon as it's made." He picked up a box of ammunition and a gun from his bench. "Here's a Colt .45—the loaner. Someone traded me that one for a new one."

"Thank you." Hoping she'd never have to use the thing, she tucked the heavy revolver under her arm and poured the brass-cased bullets into her reticule.

"Where are you staying?"

"At Culpepper's Boarding House." Captain Peele left her high and dry. "We were supposed to have an escort."

Cyrus nodded toward the station. "Need help carrying your belongings to the boarding house? Christopher probably got called out on a military exercise."

How did he know Christopher was her escort? Yet a bead of warmth spread through her. "Thank you." Nothing could go wrong. By Saturday, she'd be married to Christopher Peele and starting her new life. Although him not picking her up at the station didn't bode well.

Chapter 8

When Cyrus spied Maisie step off the train depot and cross Old Cheyenne Road, he dropped his jaw and nearly lost his footing on the roof. The raven-haired beauty crossed the street to his shop and, to his astonishment, needed him. If he thought he loved Maisie from her quick wit and intelligent humor in her letters, seeing her in person made him explode with feelings of longing and desire. He recognized her in an instant.

Yet she was another man's betrothed.

He worked on his roof to ensure Gambell and his vermin didn't sneak across the barber shop or supply company's roofs and slip down his chimney to steal any more firearms. Yet he doubted they'd be back. They got what they came for. Returning would be foolish, since Cyrus could identify them. Low-life cheaters—hitting him while he slept. The lump on the back of his head still pained him. They stole six guns—his best work. Well, one was returned. He'd like nothing more than to retrieve the other five.

After helping Miss Brinley to Eulalia Culpepper's, Cyrus worked at his bench on her handgun—a small, little six-shooter she could carry. He placed the pre-made gun springs on the bench, then he filed and sawed the frame. As he worked, he remembered her sweet words and their playful banter. What should he place in the handles? Silver? Nothing was too good for her, but was the precious metal too much for another man's wife? How about mother-of-pearl? Delicate and decorative, yet not too expensive. He loved the colors and the swirl of the ocean found in the shells. He'd love to see the ocean one day. If it produced something this inspiring, it must be beautiful.

Speaking of beautiful…He smiled at the thought of Miss Maisie using that old flintlock. The muzzleloader was at least a hundred years old. She was lucky she didn't bust the whole thing or set herself on fire with so much powder. Burns were still noticeable on her dress, and her hair held a tinge of sulfur. A blessed angel must've been watching over her was all he could figure.

Using his old bellows, he stoked the coke on his forge. Even though he owned a hand-crank, he still preferred the rhythm of the foot bellows and the wheezing of the air through the two chambers and reinstalled it.

He heated steel to harden it, just to the right temperature. After it glowed to a nice deep purple, he bent to quench the steel in the slack tub. When the metal hit the limewater, a hiss sounded. Steam rose out of the water. He added ground limestone to purify the steel. As he filed the edges of the action pieces to work the firing mechanism, he lost himself to all other thought. This was what he loved about his work. He focused on the detail, and everything else disappeared. He gave himself to the rhythm of the file, shaping the pieces he needed.

Maisie Brinley was in town! His heartbeat rose to a canter. Tremors ran to his fingers. In four days, Saturday, the fifth of July, she'd marry Christopher

Peele who grew no thoughts in his head that someone else hadn't planted there. Cyrus ground his teeth. She deserved better.

The door swung open, flooding the small shop with sunlight and July heat.

Captain Peele stood in the doorway. "She's here!"

"I know." He didn't admit she had been in his shop and commissioned him to fix her family heirloom or that the very metal he tempered was for her gun. "Where were you?"

He removed his tan, felted hat and dropped it to the counter. With both hands, he hid his face. "I couldn't face her. I chickened out. I can't do this." Captain Peele grasped the counter for support. "I can't. I can't. I can't." Between each breath, he sucked in more air. "She'll find out I'm a fraud, and then what? Will she leave? Worst case scenario, I leave town, and she goes home to Boston, right?"

Christopher inhaled so deeply and so often, Cyrus was afraid he would suck away all the air from his forge. He picked up a slack bucket and dumped it over his friend's head.

Sputtering, Christopher swiped at his eyes. "Why did you dump water over me?" His blue wool uniform turned darker from the wet. The brass buttons shone.

Cyrus dropped the bucket and placed his hands on his hips. "You looked about to explode. Listen, this woman made great effort and many sacrifices to come here. She left home and family to travel to Wylder. You could have at least met her at the station."

Running a hand through his hair, Christopher paced. "I can't talk to her. The moment I open my mouth, she'll know I didn't write all those letters."

Cyrus smiled inwardly. He'd love to see that moment.

Christopher paused. "Do you think she was mad I didn't meet her at the station?"

She should've been spitting mad, but instead she forgave him. "She came here. I told her you were called out to a military exercise."

"You're the best friend." Christopher closed his eyes and held out his hands and pressed his palms together. "Thank you for covering for me." He opened his eyes and snatched up his hat. "Is she pretty?"

Cyrus drew a deep breath. Words failed him in her description. Her dark hair fell in silken coils around her neck. Her eyes flashed when she told the story of shooting the train robbers. Her smile sent his heart to the top of his chest. "Yes, she's pretty."

Christopher slapped his hat against his hand. "Yahoo! I knew she had to be! Where is she now?"

He nearly slobbered all over himself like a puppy. Cyrus inhaled. "She's at the boarding house, I suspect."

Taking a step forward, Christopher raised his eyebrows. "Do you think I should go over there?"

Cyrus shrugged, yet his stomach turned at the thought of them together.

"How fast do you think I can kiss her?"

Christopher gripped the edge of the counter as if he held the reins of a horse in a full gallop. Cyrus rolled his eyes. Christopher didn't deserve her. But Maisie would never go for a guy like Cyrus. He didn't dare lift his thoughts to her. Although his thoughts were often on her and the witty things she wrote. "Put off your visit a little longer. Let her rest up and get settled." The last thing he wanted was for Christopher and her to be together. Cyrus needed time to sort out his feelings. What did he feel toward Maisie? He faced the bench with his back to Christopher.

"I'll go over tonight. And…" Christopher slapped his hat with the palm of his hand. "I can't talk to her. I'm afraid to say something inappropriate."

"Well, that would be everything on your mind," Cyrus murmured. He faced his friend.

Christopher's eyebrows peaked, and the color drained from his face. "Maybe you can just tell her to meet me at the church for the wedding on Saturday?" Beads of sweat broke out across his forehead.

He really looked as if he were about to toss his lunch all over the workbench. Cyrus's heart churned. "I'll help you. I've got an idea of how you can talk to her. Don't worry. Meet me tonight after the sun goes down. We'll go over and visit her together." He slapped Christopher on his soggy back. "But before you go, will you run to the water pump and fill my bucket?"

****

On Buckboard Alley, Maisie climbed the stairs and opened the door to Culpepper's Boarding House, trembling. She inhaled, bracing herself for what might come next.

Cara stood outside to guard the trunk once again.

Earlier, Cyrus lifted the trunk as if it were nothing and carried it a good pace from the train station clear to the boarding house. Impressive, for sure. Inside the house was clean and cozy. Sofas surrounded a fireplace. Stairs led off to the right. A blackboard marked the menu for the week:

Baked Beens and Biskits
Beef and Barley Stu

Lam and Potatos
Leak Soup

Maisie gripped her reticule. She had plenty of money, but she didn't know what her future held. A woman blew in with a starched, white shirt, like a sail in Boston Harbor. The rustle of her skirts sounded like the rushing of wind.

"May I help you?" The woman stood near a small wooden desk near the back of the room.

This must be Eulalia Culpepper, the proprietress—the owner of the boarding house Christopher wrote about. Her yellowing red hair was pinched into a bun in the back of her head. She flattened her eyes to little slits as her pupils inspected Maisie. Maisie ran a self-conscious hand down the front of her soiled dress. "I'm looking to rent a room for a week."

"A week, eh? What brings you to Wylder for a week?"

Her voice held a bitterness and was pinched as if she'd been sucking on lemons. Maisie thrust up her chin. She knew how to deal with these types of women. Mother managed these women with a well-placed compliment and show of wealth. Maisie didn't like flaunting her money, but for shallow people, it was the only virtue they valued.

Maisie lifted her chin higher. She oiled her voice like when Mother brought suitors for dinner—an affected, highly exaggerated expression of sophistication. "Yes, I'd like to rent your best room. Money is no object. I want my sheets cleaned twice a week with proper soap and laundering." She hefted her small purse filled with coins onto the desk.

At the jangling sound, Mrs. Culpepper widened her

eyes. She smiled. "Of course, I should've recognized a woman in a fine silk dress to want the very best."

For a flash, she was almost pretty. Maisie inwardly rolled her eyes at the flattery, especially at the mention of the silk dress she'd been wearing for longer than she'd ever worn a dress before. And she doubted Mrs. Culpepper's idea of "very best" would be anything similar to what Maisie was accustomed to. She stopped herself. That last thought was beneath her. Last week she might have been moving in circles of the Boston elite, but from now on, she would be eating baked "beens" and "biskits" for dinner. "I also need help bringing in my trunk. The kind gunsmith brought it this far."

Mrs. Culpepper bowed her head. "I'll get one of the men to bring it upstairs."

"Thank you."

The door opened behind her.

"You there, close the door. You're letting in flies."

The sudden change in tone in Mrs. Culpepper's voice made Maisie start. She turned to see who would be the object of such a tongue-lashing.

Cara stood in her simple dress near the door.

"And what do you want?" Eulalia jabbed her fists into her plump hips.

With a stern jaw, Maisie faced the proprietress. "She's with me."

Eulalia's eyes softened. "I have quarters in the back for servants. I won't charge you half as much."

Maisie raised her chin. "She's not a servant. She'll be staying in my room. With me."

Eulalia hardened her gaze again. "I'll have to charge you double."

"Money is no object." She bit her lip inside her cheek and hoped she sounded more confident than she felt. If she ran out of money, she could always wire home for Mother to send more. She tightened her grip on her reticule. No, she had to stop thinking this way. She could no longer depend on her parents. She embraced her own fate. What was a week at the best place in town? What would that cost? Soon she'd be the wife of a captain in the army, living a glorious dream.

"Follow me." Pinching her dress, Eulalia marched upstairs. "Dinner is at five p.m. sharp, and we end dinner at six. If you're not on time, you don't eat. Breakfast is six to seven."

"So early?" Maisie murmured. She followed up the squeaking wooden steps, hooking her elbow around Cara's. Staying at a boarding house was so foreign. She didn't know what to expect. A bed would feel so deliciously soft.

Eulalia opened the door.

Maisie placed a hand over her mouth. This room was no Tremont Hotel in Boston. In the room the size of her dinner table back home sat a wrought-iron bed with a sagging mattress, barely big enough for two. A worn quilt lay over the foot. Opposite the bed, on the right wall, a dressing table with a pitcher for washing and a mirror squatted in the corner. She wasn't sure her trunk would fit in the room at all. She gulped.

"Outhouse is in the back. Or you have the pot." Eulalia nodded toward the ceramic dish near the foot of the bed. "Don't dump it out the window. We're not complete barbarians out here." She flattened her lids again. "What's the matter? Not good enough for you?"

Straightening her spine, Maisie steeled herself.

"This is perfect. We thank you. Here's a little something." Maisie patted a coin into the owner's hand.

Again, Mrs. Culpepper smiled away ten years. But it quickly faded, and Eulalia retreated downstairs.

Maisie unbuttoned the top button at her neck. "I am ready for a bath, but I think we'll have to be satisfied with a small pat with a wet cloth."

Cara grinned. "I'll be happy to help ye undress."

"Oh, no." Maisie stepped away. "I told you if you came, you came as an equal. Once I am married I cannot afford to pay you salary."

With both hands, Cara grabbed her arms. "Then let me pay off me ticket and me room and board. Now, I'll help ye undress so ye can wash. We can set the room to rights after dinner."

Later that afternoon, Maisie felt a thousand times better after a nap and wash. She wore a fresh lavender silk dress and even powdered her hair with scents. As she descended for dinner, she ran a hand down the worn railing.

A crowd of men surrounded the small, bare table.

"If you're late, you don't eat." Mrs. Culpepper came in with a basket of biscuits. "Better grab a seat. Your friend better be here in one minute or she'll forfeit her meal."

"She's coming." Gulping, Maisie arched an eyebrow. The smell of baked beans and biscuits rose to her nose. She was used to eating much later. Her stomach was hardly ready for food, if you could call what was being slopped out on tin plates food. She bit her lip and found a place at the end of a rough-fashioned bench. She tucked her skirts close.

Mrs. Culpepper disappeared into the kitchen.

The adjacent man grinned. A gold tooth gleamed in the few candles set up on the sideboard and in the middle of the table.

They dripped something awful and either the candles or the man smelled of animal.

"Evening."

Though he had none on his head, salt-and-pepper-colored hair poked from his ears and nose. Maisie gulped and tried to remember her manners. "How do you do?" Keeping her movements to a minimal, she nodded. She hoped one of these men wasn't Christopher Peele. All needed a good washing and a barber. Clothes were stained with sweat around the arms. Her stomach flipped, rejecting the food. Instead of bone china and silver utensils, a metal tin plate and one spoon whittled from wood sat before her.

Men snatched biscuits from the basket. Several men spoke loudly about the days' adventures at the nearby ranches, barely chewing before swallowing and talking with food spraying from their mouths.

Mother would be horrified.

Cara, in a pink calico dress, settled across the table with a smile. She grabbed a biscuit, cut it open with a large knife, and slid butter between the two halves

She seemed to have done this a thousand times. Cara was in her element here. Maisie dropped her hands into her lap. What was she doing in Wylder? Had she made a mistake coming to Wyoming Territory? Inhaling, she picked up her wooden spoon. No, she would try to fit in. Living on the frontier was her life now.

After dinner, the sun sank behind the hills. Once back in her room, she felt her eyes sag. She plopped on the bed. "First thing in the morning, let's buy some simpler clothes. I stand out in my Boston clothes." All her lacy frills and her fine corsets felt silly here.

A tap sounded at the window.

Maisie shook her head. She must be hearing things.

Another tap.

In the middle of unpacking a corset from the trunk, Cara turned toward the window. "Did ye hear that?" She crossed the squeaking, wooden floor boards and peeked out the window. "A man is down there."

Rolling off the bed with a start, Maisie opened the window and stuck her head out of the wooden sash. A dashing man in uniform stood below them in the semi-darkness.

"Miss Maisie?"

His words sounded as smooth as warmed milk. She squinted and shifted to get a good look at his face. But only the outline of Calvary officer's hat and coat was visible in the shadow. "Yes?"

"It is I, Christopher. I am here to apologize from the bottom of my heart for not being at the station when you arrived."

His dreamy baritone voice sounded familiar, perhaps because she imagined it so many times. "I was a little put out." She crossed her arms over her chest. "I traveled for several days to see and to be with you."

His arms swung wide. Then he clasped his chest. "My heart aches at the thought I have neglected you."

She grasped the sash and thrust out her chin. "I did send a telegram from Cheyenne."

"Wild horses couldn't keep me from you."

Folding her arms across her chest, she leaned against the frame. "Wild horses couldn't keep you, yet training exercises could?"

"Uh, yes. True the exercises kept me." He paused.

Whispers sounded below. Maisie leaned out farther to hear.

His hat shadowed his face. "But my only desire is to better myself in my profession so I can care for you."

Moving away from the window, Cara wrinkled her nose and bent over the trunk. "Who wants a man who speaks so?"

Maisie turned and stuck out her tongue at Cara.

"You move with grace."

Captain Peele drew her attention back outside. Maisie leaned out the window again.

"When I first clapped eyes on you, my heart told me you were a woman with secrets. I saw the flash of intelligence in your eyes along with understanding. Your beauty fills the night. The stars—nay, the moon and sun—are jealous of your radiance. They hide their faces in shame tonight."

More whispers sounded below.

With a slow smile, Maisie strained to hear the words. When did he first clap eyes on her? Tonight?

"My heart beats only for you." His voice rose again. "But it beats me for not being near you. Come down so we may talk."

The thrill of finally meeting the man with whom she exchanged pieces of her heart was too tempting. "I'll be right down." She moved away from the window.

A swear pierced the night.

"What was that?" Maisie leaned into the darkness, trying to see though the veil of night. But his face escaped her.

He coughed. "Uh, nothing. Do, do come down. Come down, and we shall revel in this night together."

Without another word, she flashed Cara a smile. Being alone with a man after dark was not proper. A nagging thought ran through her mind. Mother's disapproving brow flashed in her head. But she had practically engaged herself to Christopher.

Tsking her tongue, Cara shook her head and arranged items in the trunk. "Yer goin' out there without a proper chaperone? What would yer mother say?"

She didn't want Cara tagging along. She thrust up her chin. "This is the Wild West, isn't it? And my mother isn't here." With a burst of excitement, Maisie slipped out of the room and down the stairs. Finally, she could meet her one true love.

Chapter 9

Drat! Again, Cyrus convinced Miss Brinley to come to Christopher. He needed to stop doing that. With trembling hands, he yanked off the hat and blue Calvary coat that barely buttoned across his chest and tossed them.

In the shadows of the boarding house, Christopher quickly fastened the brass buttons.

Under the cover of darkness, speaking his own true words, Cyrus felt a pull toward Miss Brinley. He should stop smashing his heart like a hammer on an anvil.

"Stay nearby. Don't leave me."

Christopher's eyes bugged out of his sockets. Cyrus half wanted to slap some sense into the young man. "I won't leave you, but you have everything you need in your hat. If you need words to say, take off your hat and read inside the brim." He stuck the felt hat on Christopher's head.

Nodding, Christopher gulped. He wiped his hands on his pants. "My palms are all sweaty. And I think I'm going to toss my dinner."

"Never mention bodily functions or liquids in front of a woman." Cyrus ducked into the shadows, avoiding the light shining from the front windows of the clapboard boarding house.

Miss Maisie appeared at the door. Alone!

Even backlit, she looked radiant. Cyrus dropped his

jaw, then clamped his mouth shut. Her gaze tarried on another man. Setting his jaw, he reminded himself she belonged to Christopher—the cow patty of a man. Immediately, he regretted his thoughts. Christopher was one of the few true friends Cyrus had in Wylder. He needed to learn to be happy for him.

In front of the stairs, Christopher stood in the light coming from the open door. "Miss Maisie!" His mouth slacked open. His eyes bugged out.

He trembled like a leaf. Cyrus rolled his eyes. "Say something," he whispered under his breath.

"Gosh, you are beautiful. I could bed you right now."

She furrowed her dark eyebrows. "What?"

"I mean…" Shaking, Christopher shook his head and wiped his hands on his trousers.

At last, he seemed to get possession of himself. Cyrus breathed a bit of relief.

Christopher removed his hat. "Would you like to walk in the fair evening?" With his hat, he pointed toward Buckboard Alley.

Miss Maisie beamed. "I'll grab my shawl." She slipped inside.

The door closed. Beams of moonlight streamed between the buildings.

"I did it. I did it. Did you see? I asked the question, and she said yes."

Moving into shadow, Christopher's eyes grew to the size of wagon wheels. Cyrus gave him a nod and clapped him on the shoulder. "Good boy. Now be sure to stick with the script." He ducked back into the shadows. "Don't say anything on your own, or you will have a disaster."

Miss Maisie opened the door again. A fringed shawl graced her shoulders. She delicately stepped down. Cyrus wished he could be the one to run to her.

Stepping up to Christopher, she pinched the shawl at her chest. "I am here to partake of your Wyoming. Is it not for the dreamers?"

Christopher grasped her hand at the bottom of the steps. "It's a fine night, isn't it?"

She crumpled her brow.

Christopher didn't respond to her question. She referenced Cyrus's words, and Christopher had no idea what she was talking about. Cyrus ran a trembling palm across his lips. This wouldn't end well.

Christopher held his hat at his heart. He peeked inside the rim. "The moon glows brightly tonight, but it is not as radiant as your smile."

Try not to sound too obvious, Cyrus wanted to say from his hiding spot in the shadows. She might detect he spoke someone else's words.

Miss Maisie tilted her head, but then the corners of her lips turned upward.

She stared at Christopher with eyes brighter than carriage lamps. A twinge of emotion hit Cyrus's heart. He gulped.

"Your warmth fills me with sunlight." Christopher read another line.

He wasn't supposed to read them all standing right here! Slumping against the siding, Cyrus slid a hand down the scarred side of his face.

"Tell me more," Miss Maisie cooed.

Cyrus straightened. Even with Christopher's terrible delivery, she enjoyed the words penned from his own heart? A lightness burst through his chest.

Christopher's gaze dropped to his hat. "I have waited on bated breath to hear your footsteps tread across my floor, to feel your skirts brush the timbers of my kegs…"

Maisie's smile faltered.

Cyrus rolled his eyes.

Christopher pulled his hat closer. "Uh, *legs,* and to whisper sweet nothings into your ear for your delight."

"These are indeed sweet nothings." She glanced behind her. "Perhaps we should walk away from the prying eyes of the proprietress and find someplace more private."

Bad idea. Cyrus gulped. If Christopher didn't have enough light, he couldn't read. Heck, he could barely read with good lighting.

"Let's walk." Christopher pointed with his hat and led her north, up Buckboard Alley. Then he headed west toward the plains, away from the town. A trail meandered through the sagebrush to a small ridge.

When he learned to track in the army, he mastered keeping his feet quiet. Cyrus stalked them at a safe distance. Only darkness greeted him out here. He was stunned by the stars. "Like crown jewels, they grace the heavens," he murmured to himself. He crouched along the bushes, listening.

Even in the dim light, Christopher checked his hat. He squinted and brought it close to his face. He bit his lip and glanced around.

He couldn't see the words. Panic gripped Cyrus's throat. "Words fail me in the darkness," Cyrus whispered to himself, since he knew Christopher couldn't hear him.

"Tell me about the stars."

Maisie's dark outline blotted out the stars on the horizon.

"What beautiful thoughts do you have about stars?"

Christopher visibly gulped. "The stars?"

In the moonlight, Maisie upturned her face. "The ancients believed heroes were immortalized in the stars. I wonder if I will ever do anything heroic enough to be counted among them."

Cyrus held his breath. Her words echoed his own thoughts perfectly.

"Oh, I'm sure you're heroic." Christopher patted her on the shoulder.

"Not like you, you who face danger every day as an officer."

He shrugged. "It's not really as tough as people say. Mostly I just ride around and make sure people don't drink too much."

Cyrus rolled his eyes. If anytime was the right time to talk up the captain's accomplishments, that would've been the time.

Maisie lowered her head. "We could've used you while we crossed the plains. We were attacked by train robbers. They took my wedding dress. I wish you could've been there to stop them."

Christopher guffawed. "I don't know if I could've taken on any train robbers. I barely even shoot my gun. Once, I had to shoot an old, sick buffalo that meandered into town. You should've seen it."

Shaking his head, Cyrus counted four I's in Christopher's last speech, and he didn't ask her about the robbery.

"Haven't you fought in any battles?" She raised her head again. "I heard about The Battle of Little Big

Horn. Did you ride with Custer?"

He shook his head. "Most of the men died on the battlefield. Poor Custer and his poor planning. He shouldn't have split his company in two. At least, that's what the military experts are saying now. I don't have to fight. But the uniform sure looks dashing, don't you think?" Tugging at his collar, he stood straight and grinned.

"Yes, of course." Again, Miss Maisie raised her gaze to the stars. "You are such a walking contradiction."

"Oh?"

Christopher probably didn't even know what contradiction meant.

"You write such words from your soul and yet..." She faced him. "Kiss me."

"What?" Christopher dropped his hat.

Cyrus's chest burned. His face felt afire again.

"Kiss me." Her voice rose. "If we are to be married on Saturday, we should at least find out if we have a spark. We are already a match intellectually."

Cyrus turned away. He couldn't watch. Silently, he trod the trail back to town. He only had to keep up this charade for four more days. After that, Christopher would be on his own. Cyrus just hoped he could last that long without confessing his feelings to Miss Maisie.

****

To avoid being caught by Mrs. Culpepper for missing curfew, Maisie floated upstairs in the boarding house. Her skirts swept the floorboards of her room. She sighed and leaned against the closed door to her bedroom.

Standing at the wash basin, Cara arched an eyebrow. "He kissed ye, didn't he?"

A deep warmth filled Maisie. "A woman never tells of her conquests." Joy burst through her. She floated on the feeling of connecting souls with a man of equal intelligence. She flopped on the bed, stomach down. The springs wheezed under her. Christopher's strong arms wrapped her again.

"It's well after midnight, and I doubt ye *talked* for that long."

Maisie sat up. "Oh, no, we talked." But only briefly. And Christopher only wanted to talk battle strategy. "But then we kissed." A slow smile crept on her lips, and she rolled onto her back. Had they kissed for hours? Time stood still. Only the stars and the animals of the night knew of their secret embrace. Under the beautiful canopy of stars, his warmth enveloped her and transported her. Such a better kisser than Harold Peabody, the only other man she kissed. She traced her lips with her fingers. What would her mother say?

Cara filled the water bowl and picked up the washing cloth. "I can only imagine. How did ye get back in without wakin' the missus?"

"Christopher opened a first floor window in the parlor, and I sneaked in."

"How dashing! He did look mighty fine in his uniform, did he not?"

Propping herself on her hand, she arched a brow. "Was that you peeking out the window? I thought it Mrs. Culpepper. All I caught was a flash of red hair."

"She might've been watchin', too, but I certainly caught a gander." Cara sighed and held out the cloth.

102

"To be loved by such a man."

"He was acting a little strange tonight." She traced the quilt stitches. How bizarre he didn't respond to her comment about the Wyoming being for dreamers.

Cara crushed the wash cloth against her chest. "Posh, who cares when shoulders like his are around ye."

"I consented to be his wife on Saturday. Our engagement is official." A thrill zinged up her spine. What would it be like to be married to such a dashing man?

Cara inhaled sharply. "So fast!"

Daydreaming about his lips, Maisie sat up and let her feet dangle from the bed. She passed a hand down her silk bodice. "Don't forget we'll go shopping tomorrow."

"Shopping?" Cara widened her eyes. "Of course, miss."

"And don't be calling me miss."

Winking, Cara grinned. "Of course, miss."

After her evening toilette, Maisie hugged her pillow that felt as if it had been stuffed with straw. She re-read the few remaining letters and pored over the words. She ran a finger across the ink and kissed the cursive C at the bottom. On Saturday, she would write her mother and sign it Mrs. Christopher Peele!

****

Wednesday morning, Maisie and Cara trod the boards lining the shops on Wylder Street to Mrs. Lowery's dress shop. Mrs. Culpepper said the shop was the only place in town to get a dress or to have the wash done.

In a courtyard between two brick buildings, a

woman scrubbed linens in a wooden wash basin. Lines of freshly washed clothes waved like billowing sails in the sun.

Gulping, Maisie nodded toward the young woman. Lye from the boiling pots tainted the air. "I'd hate to have to hire out laundry on a captain's income. You will show me how, won't you, Cara?" Mother never allowed her to do any menial tasks. But as the wife of a captain, she would surely have to do these chores! She hooked her elbow in Cara's arm.

"Aye." Cara cast a sideways glance. "Are ye sure ye have the skills to be a proper wife? Yer used to havin' everythin' done for ye."

"I can manage if you teach me." Maisie bit her lip.

"Lye will make your hands rough, as will scrubbing pots and plucking chickens."

Plucking chickens? Her stomach turned. She hadn't thought about food! "I'll have to cook? I have so much to learn." None of her upbringing prepared her to tend her own household. She knew how to play the piano, read and write, manage servants, and how to pour and serve tea for guests. Why hadn't Mother taught her important skills like how to cook or do laundry? She gulped. Being the mistress of her own house sounded hard.

"Aye. But yer a smart lass, and ye'll get on just fine." Patting her hand, Cara cast a smile.

Maisie stepped out of the sun into the cool shadow of Widow Lowery's shop. She crumpled her brow at the plain, cotton print dresses. The displayed fashions were years out of date. She pinched a corner of fabric. And rough and thickly woven, too. Back in Boston, Mr. Prentice from Yardley's dropped everything to wait upon Maisie and Mother. He even issued house calls for fittings.

In the back of the shop, two women talked loud enough to be overheard. The first, who Maisie assumed was Mrs. Lowery because of the measuring tape around her neck, swept back graying hair into a wisp of a bun. She hitched up glasses perched on the end of her nose.

Another lady in a maroon walking dress, with a black, velvet collar and matching bonnet, stood next to her and nodded.

Mrs. Lowery's expression soured. She pinched her wrinkled lips and tsked.

"And I told her, if her daughter wanted to find herself a respectable husband, she should stop hanging around those Holland boys from up north. I've heard stories about them that would turn your hair white—swearing, drinking, and all sorts of other debaucheries. And I heard one of them is a writer. Imagine, a writer of those horrid novels."

She narrowed her eyes, her face as wrinkled as freshly washed cotton Maisie couldn't believe the close-minded comments. She thought Boston was bad—Wylder women were worse gossips.

Mrs. Lowery nodded. "I tell you, writing is the devil's work, right there. Novels will turn a soul to Satan faster than the drink."

"I'll pray for her." The other lady leaned in and patted Mrs. Lowery's hand.

She, too, had a pinched expression as if she drank bath water. Maisie eyed them from the side of the shop while she looked at fabric, biting her lips to remain silent.

"Yes, we sure will." Mrs. Lowery stretched out her

hand. "Can I help you?"

When Maisie realized Mrs. Lowery addressed her, she stepped back at the abrupt change in topic. "I'm looking for something suitable to wear around town." She crossed the shop to the two women.

Adjusting her glasses, Mrs. Lowery evaluated her from tip to tail. "I don't have much that's as fancy as what you're wearing."

Maisie swept a hand over her silk skirt. "I prefer something much more serviceable—cotton and plain. And I am in need of a wedding dress. Could you provide one by Saturday?"

"For a price." Narrowing her eyes, Mrs. Lowery lifted an eyebrow. "We'll see what we can do. We have some ready-to-wear skirts and tops that will only need a bit of tailoring to fit."

After a morning of measurements, fitting, and adjustments, Maisie thanked Mrs. Lowery for her new cotton skirt and blouse and made arrangements for Mrs. Lowery's seamstress to sew a wedding dress for Saturday and paid extra for the tight timeline. Sickness washed over her thinking that somewhere someone benefited from her silk, Paris gown.

Cara held open the door for Maisie.

In her new, practical clothes, Maisie reached the threshold.

"Well, I never saw anyone put on such airs before." Mrs. Lowery spoke deep in the shop. "Who does she think she is walking around in silk with a maid following her like a barnyard cat?"

Maisie froze. Her chest burned. Was Mrs. Lowery talking about her, within her hearing? Maisie straightened her spine and spun. Insulting her was one thing. Calling Cara a cat was another! Maisie flooded her chest with air. That Lowery woman deserved a good tongue-lashing.

Cara placed a gentle hand on her wrist. "We're not in Boston, miss," she whispered. "Yer reputation here will follow ye. Yer money will not protect ye from gossips. Don't let them see ye hurt. 'Tis like blood to a hound."

Staring at Mrs. Lowery, Maisie bit hard until her jaw hurt. She exhaled through her nose.

Mrs. Lowery challenged through slitted eyes.

Maisie's tongue was her greatest asset, her sharpest sword, and her highest wall. She drew breath. She couldn't help herself. "You think you're so holy putting down other people with seemingly good intentions to pray for them. The Good Lord himself walked with sinners. He didn't judge them. He'd do the same if He were here today, you hypocrite. And another thing, I'd rather have airs and a maid than be a middling gossip!" Without checking Mrs. Lowery's reaction, Maisie thrust up her chin and swept from the store as if she were Mother and sailed across the boards outside. A tight smirk crossed her lips. She gave Mrs. Lowery a proper Boston chiding. If she'd had the presence of mind or read the Bible recently, she would've included a verse in there, too. She shrugged. Couldn't win them all.

Cara frowned.

No, her expression was worse than a frown. Her face crumpled in reproach.

"Ye ought not to have said that, miss."

Guilt flashed in Maisie's stomach. "Why not?"

"'Twill be but water on an oil fire, miss."

Maisie's tongue felt like a sack of flour, heavy and dry.

"Yer not Mrs. Brinley's daughter out here. Yer Captain Christopher Peele's betrothed. Any shame ye bring on yerself, ye'll bring on him."

Pain stabbed Maisie in the stomach.

"Back in Ireland, me mother always said, ye'll not make friends with vinegar, but with honey. We poor folk have to guard our names. We bow and scrape the knee to get the shop owners to wait upon us. Perhaps the rich and fair can give offense, but when ye live in a wee town on a wee income, ye will have to cultivate all the friends ye can. Ye'll live the rest of yer life here. Think of the damage ye've done." A smile parted her lips. "And besides, ye don't want to be enemies with the only dressmaker in town, do ye?"

Cara's words pricked Maisie's heart, yet she wasn't quite willing to admit fault. "I can always go to Cheyenne." Deep in her soul, she hoped she had not wounded Captain Peele. A weight suffocated her. She needed to ease her burdened heart. "Let's inquire at the gunsmith's where Captain Peele is, or if he has made any progress on the musket, shall we?"

"I have no desire to visit the disfigured gunsmith. Ye can see him tomorrow." Cara shouldered the brown paper package with the silk dress and other clothes. "We should return home and drop off ye new clothes."

Nodding, Maisie hoped her comment to the dressmaker wouldn't come back to haunt her.

Chapter 10

Thursday morning, Cyrus banged with vigor at his anvil. He couldn't put a finger on what bothered him, but something gnawed at his mind. He didn't want to search for the emotion too hard; he was afraid of what he might find.

Behind him, the door opened and closed.

Looking up at the visitor, Cyrus caught his breath. He stilled his tongs and hammer. Miss Maisie entered his shop dressed more plainly than what she wore Tuesday. The robin's-egg blue complemented her complexion. Smiling, he gulped away his desire. He nodded toward her. "If you don't mind, leave the door open." He couldn't be alone with another man's betrothed. "I can't believe back East you'd be allowed to be alone in a shop with a man."

"Back East, a shop would have more than one man." A tinge of pink rose to her cheeks as she opened the door again, letting the sunshine spill on the dirt floor.

"I see you've visited the local dress shop." He tried to keep the scarred side of his face away from her. But both eyes begged to look.

She glanced down and pulled out her skirt. "I thought it more appropriate to dress like the locals. I traded in my silks for this." Smiling, she held out her skirt and spun. "What do you think?"

He examined the curves of her dress. "You know, I might like this look better than your Boston clothes."

Maisie's cheeks tinted pink again. "I've come to inquire about the musket."

A thrill shook him. He couldn't help but smile. "You must think I'm a miracle worker, Miss Brinley. I told you that piece wouldn't be ready for a week. However, I am almost done with your new gun."

"Can I see it?" Her eyes grew large as she leaned over the counter.

His heart leaped. Hooking a thumb in his apron, he shook his head. "Ah-ah. I am afraid not. I don't let any of my customers view the work before it's done." He pointed with his tongs. "To do so is bad luck, you know." The sound of her laughter sent shivers down his spine. A fire stoked in his heart.

"Where's Christopher?" She glanced around the shop.

Like hot steel in a slack tub, the fire was out. He turned to his work and hit more metal. "He went off to catch arsonists. Someone set brush fires up north. They can be dangerous." He faced her. "The wind carries the flame across miles of scrub trees and sagebrush, and the fire destroys whole towns."

"Will he be safe?"

"As safe as one can be out here. Wyoming Territory is wild country, Miss Brinley. If you want safety, you won't find it here."

Nodding, she plucked at something in her hand. "Will he be away often?"

"Likely. I'm afraid riding the range is the life of an officer." He banged until his forearms hurt. A tickle of perspiration pricked his skin.

"Is gun-making hard?"

Turning, he grinned. He wiped sweat off his forehead with his sleeve. "Hard? No, but lots of different pieces go into constructing one."

She cocked her head to the side. "What made you decide to be a gunsmith?"

A flash of memory hinted at the edges of his mind. He stood with Meade's men on Cemetery Ridge. Death and blood surrounded him. The smell of sulfur burned his nose. But he shoved aside the memory. "Well, making guns is more interesting than sharpening plow shares or shoeing horses. My father was a blacksmith, but he encouraged me to refine my skills." Though Paw passed years ago, those formative times in his shop shaped him. Paw recognized Cyrus's attention to detail, and Cyrus was always grateful he led him in the right direction. "So after the war, I searched out a gunsmith in Utah. Great man. You might have heard of his son— John Moses. He was brilliant even at age ten—when I first met him."

"You really went to the Utah Territory and lived with the Mormons?" Maisie leaned over the bench. Her eyes widened.

"Sure." He hit the steel again, but his effort was for effect. He doused the steel. It no longer held his attention. The water steamed and hissed. Wiping his hands, he faced her.

Leaning back, she chuckled. "Wha-hoo, what would my mother say about that!" She fanned herself with a handkerchief.

A smile blossomed on her lips. Cyrus replaced his tongs to distract himself from thinking about her lips. "Jonathan took me on as an apprentice for three years and treated me as a son. I was in his shop when John Moses made his own gun design. He's awaiting his patent. It should be filed sometime this year. They're really nice folks."

Maisie dropped her smile. "I'm sure they are. I'm sorry. I meant no disrespect to your friends. But so many wives!"

"I only need one." Grinning, he leaned against his workbench and crossed his arms.

She tilted her head. "What would you envision your life like with your one wife?"

Her dark blue eyes squinted when she smiled. Cyrus caught his breath. "Oh, I dunno." He focused on the tool and picked up the hammer. "We'd live on our little homestead outside of town. We'd hear the sounds of laughter all throughout our cozy, comfortable home. We'd gather the children and read good works like the Bible and Shakespeare. I can see us circling the hearth, fighting over who gets to hold the big book and read aloud to the rest of us. Or maybe we'd dramatize the scenes." He envisioned his future with a dark-haired woman at his side, working alongside one another. Twirling the hammer, he glanced up. Maisie's gaze was riveted to his.

Her lips parted slightly.

"Sorry." Heat rose from his collar. "That was more than what you wanted to hear."

Taking a deep breath, she cleared her throat. "What do you like about gunsmithing?"

Relieved to change the subject, he dropped his hammer to his bench. "It's an art. I take raw materials and create a something never made before. I love the fine details. I can spend months carving antlers into a pastoral scene for grips. The other smiths don't do that. Smithing might sound the same to you, but the amount of detail for creating a gun far surpasses anything else."

She examined some of his display pieces. "As I said before, they are beautiful."

"Thank you." The compliment warmed him. The desire to create burst through him. He couldn't wait to show her the gun he crafted for her.

"Someday, I'd like to try."

"Really?" A spark ran up his spine.

A grin broke out across her lips. "Smithing can't be more difficult than sewing. And my mother constantly made me attend to my needlework."

"I'll teach you sometime." But even as he said it, he knew showing her his craft wouldn't happen. Inhaling, he tucked in his lips. Come Saturday, she would be another man's wife.

"You can teach me now, if you'd like."

She placed her hands behind her back and swung her dress from her hips like a bell. The gesture sent his heart slamming into his ribs.

"I'm not doing anything." She dropped her reticule to the counter.

Cyrus's heartbeat kicked up. The faintest desire of her heart was his command. He shouldn't. But he couldn't help himself. "Come around the counter. I don't have an extra apron. You might get your new clothes dirty."

She stepped around the counter. "I don't mind."

So near, he smelled the scent of lavender fields. He gulped down the tremors rising in his throat. "Well, first let me tell you about the coal forge. You want smaller sized pieces, about the size of a pea for the

113

heart of your fire. You gather your coke into an area here with your rake." He stroked the coke and stirred the fire to make it glow. "Then you breathe life into it by giving it air. You can step on the foot bellows here."

Miss Maisie stepped close enough.

Her skirts brushed his leg. A shot of lightning ran through his body.

She hesitated. With a deep blush, she held up her skirts just a little to pump the bellows. "Like this?"

"Exactly so." At her modesty, a flame burst up through the center of his heart. "Then you grab your steel and dig it in there." He placed a rod of steel in the coal.

"How long do you leave it?" She peeked over his shoulder.

He grasped the steel with tongs. "Each color is a different temperature. You wait until steel burns to purple for what we're doing."

"The metal truly turns purple?" Her eyes widened.

Right now it burned a brilliant yellow. "Indeed. But it takes time. You have to make sure it's the right temperature, or the metal will be too brittle, and it will snap like glass."

A smile graced her lips. She stared into the coals. "Oh, I can't wait to see."

She stood near his shoulder. His heart raced at having her near. He examined her through the corner of his eye. Her profile was so delicate. Such a lovely nose and her lips curled into a sweet bow. Her dark hair was the color of soot. He wanted to ask her about what she meant about being heroic, but then he remembered she spoke those words to Christopher, not him.

"I thought I might find you here." Christopher

stood in the door.

Cyrus jumped and separated himself from her. Then he realized Christopher spoke to Miss Maisie, not Cyrus. A dull ache throbbed in his heart. While with her, he'd forgotten about his ugly scar—his disfigured face. Now it burned even hotter.

Maisie stepped away from the fire and from Cyrus. "Good morning!" She crossed the shop. "I've been waiting for you."

At last, the steel glowed a royal purple, and with tongs, Cyrus picked it up from the coal and quenched it in the slack tub with a hiss. Could he squelch his feelings for her?

****

Taking Captain Peele's proffered elbow, Maisie crossed the dirt floor toward the gunsmith shop exit. "I almost forgot. We were supposed to report the stolen gun to the sheriff's office."

"What?" Captain Peele stepped back.

His blond hair was a little mussed from taking off his hat inside. He was lean and not nearly as muscular as Cyrus. And Cyrus was always a gentleman. He even asked her to keep the door open. Christopher could learn a thing or two from his friend. She swiveled to face Cyrus. "I promised I'd report the stolen gun to the sheriff. Cyrus said he'd take me. He said he knew who robbed the train."

Cyrus raised his head from the bench.

She could see only his good side. He was ruggedly handsome. He was older than the captain by a few years. Yet, not a single gray hair graced his dark mane. His shoulders, although hunched at the moment, were broad and powerful—much more powerful than

Christopher's.

Cyrus straightened. "I'd be happy to escort you over to the sheriff's office and offer my testimony as well."

He brought his gaze to Maisie's. She felt such depth in his eyes—such soul. Even without words he communicated his gratitude. Somehow she felt his emotion rather than hear his words.

"We'll all go." Captain Peele coughed. "I have to put up my horse. I'll meet you over there." He backed out of the shop.

Afraid Cyrus would see into the depths of her heart, Maisie lowered her gaze. "Why does he always avoid me?"

Cyrus wiped his hands on a bit of cotton. "You make him nervous."

"I do?" She raised her gaze.

He nodded.

"Do you think he'll get used to me once we are married?" She imagined her whole life persuading her husband not to shake or tremble in her presence—or not to run away.

Removing his leather apron, Cyrus furrowed his brow. "I don't know."

"Well, I hope he doesn't run away on our wedding night."

His cheeks tinged pink as he strapped on his holster.

Heat rose from her collar. "I mean, the eve of our wedding—the ceremony, I mean. I'm so afraid to be stood up."

"Why is that?" He gathered his hat and hung the apron on a hook.

Cyrus was so easy to talk to, as if he were an old friend. Things she hadn't ever even told Mother rose to the surface. "I had a bad experience once with a fiancé."

He grabbed a ring of keys. "Oh? Your confession surprises me. What happened?"

She fiddled with her reticule and focused on the dirt floor in front of the door, her back to him. "My experience was not a pleasant encounter. I'm sure you wouldn't want to hear it."

"I would listen to any painful experience if it took the sting from you."

He spoke low over her shoulder. The breath of his words whispered against her neck. Chills ran down her arms. His words were fresh air to her suffocated soul.

"They say sharing a burden helps lighten the load."

Why was she trembling? "I have always believed that as well." Stepping out into the sunshine, she stilled her hands and drew breath. "I fear my story is silly." Daylight pierced her eyes after being in the dark shop.

Jangling his keys, Cyrus locked up. "Go on." He headed toward Sidewinder Lane.

Strolling beside him, she felt entirely comfortable speaking about this painful subject. "Well, I was engaged to the very fashionable, very well-received Master Harold Peabody from an old Boston family. He owns several homes, five carriages, buys and sells businesses, and makes himself and others wealthy. My mother thought him the perfect match. He had red hair and freckles and an ego bigger than the..." She searched for something big enough. "The Mississippi River."

With a hand on his gun belt, Cyrus chortled.

"Okay."

"Well, one day I called on him to show him a part of my trousseau Mother and I purchased for our wedding." She lowered her voice. "Through the gossamer curtains of his townhouse, I spied him with a maid on his lap, kissing and giggling." The image still burned in her mind and in her heart. Seeing him, her betrothed, with another woman on his lap cut her to the core, not because she loved him deeply, but because she expected loyalty.

"A maid as in...?"

"A servant." She squinted her eyes against the sun. "I'm not sure the servant played a willing part. Some men use whatever power to their advantage in both business and their, *ahem*, personal lives, yet..." Heat rose to her cheeks.

"His disloyalty stung."

She faced him. He understood completely. "Yes. Sadly, even if Mother wanted to hear the truth, she would've insisted I marry him. She refused to hear what he had done. Needless to say, I canceled the engagement." Perhaps Father would've listened, but he hadn't been right since he came back from the war.

"Did you ever talk to him about it?"

"Who, Harold? Yes." She gulped. "Harold knew I wouldn't spread his misdeed around Boston society. He was right. So I gave him a tongue-lashing he never forgot. In fact, when he did marry, he married a girl of sixteen who would never stand up to him. Diantha Chaffee—Peabody, now." She shook her head. Her only comfort in the whole affair was seeing Harold cower at her words. How powerful she felt. How justified she was. "Ever since then I've been afraid to marry the wrong person. I want to be sure."

Cyrus nodded toward her. "And you're sure your Christopher is the right one?"

She lifted her chin. After reading his letters, she cemented her love and devotion to him. "Nothing is clearer in my mind."

He focused forward.

After few heartbeats passed, she brushed an errant curl from her lips. "He is a good man, isn't he?"

"The best and the luckiest of men." He stopped in front of the sheriff's office. "Here we are."

Footprints sounded in the dirt behind her. She turned.

Christopher marched toward the office, his fists clenched, face red. "Did you tell-off Mrs. Lowery?"

A deep heat flashed in her face. "Yes."

He threw up his hands. "She just hailed me from her shop and said I should teach my future wife to be more submissive."

"Submissive? The very idea!" She dared not peek at Cyrus. She didn't want to see disapproval in his eyes. Maisie bowed her head, studying the ground beneath her feet. "She had it coming." Pain throbbed in her chest.

"She says she will not make your wedding dress." Captain Peele pointed to his chest. "And not only that, you've embarrassed me!"

Snapping up her head, Maisie stamped a foot. "And I paid in advance, too. That insolent shrew! How dare she? If she shall not make the dress, whatever shall I do?"

Cyrus placed a hand on her wrist. "Don't worry. We'll find something. If we have to dispatch a wire to

Cheyenne, we'll get you a dress."

She slumped her shoulders, aching inside. But this feeling of regret wasn't about the dress. She hurt because she'd hurt her love. Cara was right. Maisie would have to learn to curb her tongue.

Captain Peele pinched his lips together. "You embarrassed me, Miss Maisie." He shook his head. His lips thinned to a straight line. Raising his hat, he nodded. "I'll see you back at the boarding house." He turned and stalked up the street, leaving puffs of dirt in his footsteps.

Her stomach turned. She wanted to cover her face and run to her room and cry. She realized Cyrus still had his hand on her wrist. Strength poured from his touch.

He nodded toward the office. "Let's go talk to the sheriff. Don't worry about him. He always cared too much about what other people think. Don't let old gossips bother you."

"But I've shamed him." Tears ached behind her eyes.

Cyrus shook his head. "He can only be embarrassed if he cares what Mrs. Lowery thinks. That old woman had a good tongue-lashing coming. She needs to mind her own business. People are like stones in a river; if they aren't turned, they grow moss. And she is one grossly green rock." He grinned. "You'll turn a few stones in Wylder, that's all. Christopher will have to accept the way you are." His gaze fell to his hand on her wrist. He dropped his grip. "Anyway, we best get inside." He gestured toward the sheriff's office.

At his words, a measure of comfort swept over her.

Cyrus opened the door.

She glanced back to where Christopher fled. Why didn't *he* comfort her?

Chapter 11

"Gambell and his band are probably long gone by now." Cyrus stepped out of the sheriff's office. The afternoon sun glared in his eyes. Wind swept in from the hills with a hint of chill. He rested his hand on his gun belt.

Near him on the boards, Maisie earnestly searched his gaze. "You don't think the constable will catch them?"

He grinned at her term for the law. Constables usually worked in a small jurisdiction. "I doubt it. If they were smart, Gambell's men will be down in Texas or up in Canada." If Cyrus ever caught up with them, he'd give them a bigger thrashing than last time. First, they stole his guns, then they threatened Miss Brinley. He set his teeth against them. If they ever showed up in Wylder again, they'd feel more than the butt of a gun, they'd feel the hot lead of his rod.

"My, what a severe expression you have." She clutched her handbag.

Cyrus hadn't realized he was scowling. He fixed his expression to be more pleasant.

"Would you mind escorting me to the boarding house?" She held out her elbow.

With a nod, he took her arm. "My pleasure." He was aware of her every move. Keeping his steps slow, he savored each step at her side.

A paper blew by. Bending, he snatched it up. "Looks like the town is having a dance Friday night to celebrate Independence Day."

She clapped her hands. "Oh, how fun. Are you planning to attend?"

He stuck out his elbow and resumed walking. "Noooo. I rarely go to social activities." He certainly didn't want to watch Miss Maisie dance with Christopher.

She whirled to face him. "Why not?"

For more than a few paces, he chewed her question. "I don't like dances."

"You don't like to dance, or you don't like the social gathering."

"Neither." He grinned.

"I sense a story."

Too many people swarmed the front steps of the Wylder Mercantile for a private conversation. "Would you like to see a herd of bison?"

She grinned. "I'd love to."

Quickening his pace, he led her up Wylder Street out past the buildings to the ridge where she and Christopher kissed. A sickening feeling boiled inside at the thought of that first night. But an urge to share grew within him even if he couldn't tell her how he felt.

Once he cleared from all the people and buildings, he pointed to the edge of a small ridge. "See that." He pointed across the plains. Dark spots crowded the horizon, moving almost as one.

"Amazing!" She held her bonnet against the wind.

"They're sure beautiful." He gulped dry air. He'd never told anyone this secret. Telling Miss Maisie seemed right. Only this time, he couldn't hide his feeling behind the pages of another man. "You want to know why I don't attend many social events?" He reached up and touched the left side of his face. "This scar."

She brushed a stray hair from her face. Tilting her head, she raised her eyebrows. "What about it?"

He smiled. "No woman would want to dance with this." Sweeping his hand, he grabbed a few sprigs of sagebrush and tore off the leaves from the stem.

"Tell me, how did you get it?"

She didn't disagree. Maybe he kind of hoped she would contradict him. His mouth as dry as the pebbles beneath his feet. Despite his best efforts, his heartbeat kicked up. Nerves ran through his hands. "I, uh." He shook.

Miss Maisie placed a hand on his forearm. "It's fine. Take your time."

Confidence flowed into him. He drew a breath. "When I was sixteen, I enlisted in the Northern Army in my hometown of Mauch Chunk, Pennsylvania. They sent me to the front."

A small gasp escaped her lips. "So young?"

He swallowed around his dry tongue. "I was highly motivated. I felt strongly against slavery and the South's secession. I had to do something." One of his closest friends, James, was enslaved in the South. As a freeman, he came to live with them and told him terrible stories of how families were split and sold and worse.

She arched a brow. "The legal age of enlistment is eighteen."

He focused on the purple horizon. "I lied to the recruiting officer. They didn't care. I looked old enough to shave. I've always been tall for my age and strong." He slid a smile in her direction. "Much like you, I borrowed my father's old flintlock inherited from his grandfather who fought in the Revolution. I ran away from home and enlisted without his consent."

Miss Maisie parted her lips, her eyes wide.

He dropped his gaze to the sagebrush near his feet. "Well, in my first battle alongside General Meade, in 1863, near Gettysburg, grown men became frightened and ran away." The smell of blood and vomit haunted him. Sulfur tinged the air. Horses galloped. Canons fired. Men yelled. "Chaos was all around. I snatched up my powder horn and poured powder into the flash pan and fired. The whole thing lit up. My face caught fire, and I was blind in my eye for two weeks. The gun hadn't been cleaned for years, and the black powder rusted out the screws. I was lucky I wasn't killed for my ignorance." He paused. "While I recovered in the infirmary listening to death, dying, and suffering all around me, with my face bandaged to where I couldn't see, I lay there and thought and prayed that if I ever lived through the war, I would learn everything about guns and teach other people to be safe. Thankfully, my eyesight returned. I was ignorant, and my ignorance nearly killed me." The Battle of Gettysburg was one of General Meade's biggest victories and a turning point in the war. Luckily, he recovered and served two more years until the conflict ended.

"What happened after the war?"

He huffed. He left Mauch Chunk a starry-eyed sixteen-year-old, naïve and brave. He finished his duty to his country at eighteen, war-weary and disfigured. "I returned to civilian life and to my sweetheart, Lucy. We planned to marry at the end of my service. Lucy took one look at my face and broke the engagement. Heartbroken, I traveled west, worked as an apprentice to Jonathan in Utah for a few years, and came here to make a living." He was as far away from women as possible. If the odds were not in his favor, then he couldn't be rejected by women. But then he met Miss Maisie. He never wanted anyone more.

She shifted and lifted her chin. "Just because one woman rejected you doesn't mean all women will. You should still come to the dance. Friday is Independence Day. The whole town will be celebrating."

"I need dancing lessons, Miss Maisie. I don't know how to waltz." While other young men his age went to dances, he fought a war. "I can't go to a dance unless I know how." He held his breath. "Would you teach me? I bet you're the best dancer in Boston."

She blushed to the tips of her raven hair.

He found her reaction charming.

Clutching her reticule in both hands in front of her skirt, she rocked forward onto her toes. "Believe it or not, the drawing rooms back home are filled with far superior dancers. However, I will teach you, if you promise to come."

Despite their deep blue color, her eyes shone. A burbling sensation he hadn't felt in a long time filled his stomach. He grinned. She positively bewitched him. "I promise to come."

"All right then. Dancing lessons begin now." She held out her palm. "First, take my hand."

He did so. Her hands felt butter-soft, like kid leather.

"And place your other hand here." She led his hand

to the curve of her waist.

With galloping heartbeat, he drew her near. The scent of her lavender soap reached his nose. The warmth of her flesh beneath his hand intrigued him. Everything felt right with her in his arms.

With her free hand, she lifted her skirts. "Step to the left."

He obliged her. She moved with grace and skill in his arms—effortlessly, as if dancing with the help of marionette strings.

"Now to the right."

Billowing clouds of glory burst through his chest, bright and sunny as bright as dawn. He spun and caught her closer. Their gazes met. Her breath whispered across his face. How he wanted to lean in and—

"I told ye they were out here. I saw them head this way."

Miss Maisie's red-headed friend rounded the bushes.

Christopher was on her heels.

Dropping her like a hot rod of steel, Cyrus jumped away from Miss Maisie. "She was just teaching me how to waltz." The clouds in his soul evaporated.

Miss Maisie colored to the tips of her ears. She brushed an errant wisp of hair away from her downcast eyes. "The town is holding a dance at the school Friday night."

The red-headed young woman clapped her hands. "A dance? How exciting! Will ye be goin', Captain Peele?"

Christopher hadn't yet spoken. His gaze focused directly on Miss Maisie, his jaw set.

A deep burning grew in Cyrus's chest. He focused

on the horizon beyond Miss Maisie, studying her profile.

At last, Miss Maisie raised her head. "You've met Cara?"

Cyrus bowed. He wasn't sure if she questioned Christopher or himself. He met her briefly while carrying the trunk to the boarding house but wasn't formally introduced.

Christopher shook his head.

Miss Maisie snagged the girl around the arm and squeezed it. "Cara is my friend from Ireland," she proclaimed with a huge grin. "She gave up a very nice position in Boston to come to Wylder. I hope you'll both dance with her to repay her selflessness."

Cara beamed at Miss Maisie and then at Christopher.

Nodding, Cyrus regretted his oath of going to the dance. What made him be so rash? In all the years he'd lived here, he rarely graced any kind of town meeting and especially one with dancing. But he'd promised Miss Maisie, and he couldn't break a vow to her, could he?

****

Friday morning dawned. Maisie pinched her eyes against the thin, cotton curtains barely offering any shade from the morning light. Breakfast was over an hour ago, she was sure. Mrs. Culpepper ordered breakfast at such inhuman hour. She tossed in bed. The springs groaned beneath her. Going back to sleep would be impossible. Small tickles of delight fluttered in her belly. Tonight was the dance. Cyrus promised to come. She sat up and hugged the quilt close to her chest.

At the bureau, Cara was already awake and starting

her toilette. She poured water into the basin and folded a towel. "Ye look a might happy. Must be because yer only one sunrise away from yer weddin' day."

Maisie's heart burned. *Oh, yes.* Her wedding to Captain Peele. She should be excited. "This is my last day as a single lady. Let's visit the festivities and make a day of it—pie contests, shooting contests, and end with a dance and fireworks!"

A pout blossomed on Cara's lips. "But I don't have anything to wear to the dance."

Maisie slid from the warmth of the bed. "Oh, Cara, wear my peach silk dress." She couldn't withhold her best dress from her best friend. After all, Cara was still single and available. Maisie was spoken for.

A sickening feeling grew at the bottom of her stomach. When she thought of Christopher, she pinched her lip and furrowed her brow. If only she had more of his letters. She needed the assurance of his love. Curse that wretched bandit who stole her wedding dress and parts of her heart.

Cara dropped open her bowed lips. "I can wear the peach silk dress?" She clasped her hands to her chest. "Bless ye, miss."

"You're not to call me miss, remember?" Maisie studied her reflection in the mirror. She couldn't understand why she looked so much prettier today. A smile in her heart wanted to burst through. Nothing could go wrong today. Tonight was the celebration.

"But Cyrus calls ye Miss Maisie."

"Cyrus? Who's that?" A flush crept to her face. She didn't want Cara to know she knew his first name. Such intimacy wouldn't be permitted in Boston. "Oh, Mr. Haddock? He's just a gentleman. He calls everyone by a title." She wasn't entirely sure she was speaking the truth, but the hope of it rang in her heart.

"No." She shook her head. "Yer the only one I've heard him call miss."

"You only met him last night."

She thrust up her chin. "But I've seen him around town. I've seen how he interacts with other women. He stares at ye from the corner of his eyes when he thinks yer not watchin'."

Hiding a smile, Maisie tied a ribbon in her hair. "Oh, posh. Cyrus is nearly thirty-two."

"And how do ye know his age?"

Hitching up her night dress, Maisie pulled it over her head. "He told me he enlisted in the army at sixteen. I simply did the math."

"Sharin' secrets, are ye?" She squinted her eyes and tilted her head.

"No, I asked him about his scar—"

"When I took the wash to Lowery's, I heard Mizz Lowery say she thinks Cyrus is taken with ye."

Maisie frowned, but secretly, she warmed at the compliment. "Mrs. Lowery is an old gossip."

Cara pinched the shoulders of Maisie's dress and held it up. "And from what I hear, he's never told anyone about his scar. Most people are afraid to even ask. In fact, he usually gets rather violent if ye mention it." She blinked.

Inhaling, Maisie propped a hand on her hip. "The insinuation in your voice astounds me."

Cara helped Maisie into her dress from Mrs. Lowery's dress shop.

Something about Cara's hinting or sly glances turned Maisie's stomach. She loved Christopher. He'd sent her the most beautiful letters filled with parts of his soul. She had to admit, she respected Cyrus. He was always the perfect gentleman. And she didn't find his scar half as appalling as when she first saw him. In fact, she barely saw it anymore.

Fitting the dress, Cara smiled. "Lots of single men live here. Yer not the only one who might end up with a weddin' ring." She stepped behind and laced up the dress. When she was done, she picked up Maisie's night clothes.

Maisie tucked in her undergarment lace under the dress at the neckline. "Oh, good!" Happiness burst through her for her friend. "I didn't know you have a beau. Have you got your eye one someone?"

Shaking out Maisie's night dress, Cara furrowed her light brows. "He doesn't even know I breathe."

Maisie rolled up her stocking onto her leg, securing it to garter clip and slid on her shoes. "Then you must do something at the dance to attract his attention. Bring him to his knee tonight." A sinking feeling nearly swamped her. Was it just an eve of wedding hesitation? She grabbed the hook and buttoned up her boots.

Once finished, she left to find Christopher and reassure herself that he was the one for her.

Stepping out into the mid-morning sun, Maisie found Christopher near the Calvary office. "Can I talk to you for a second?"

"Sure." He led her to a bench on the boardwalk shaded by a veranda. "What's on your mind?"

A knot twisted in her stomach. He looked a little less impressive in his blue cavalry jacket and his yellowed gauntlets today. "You know how I told you bandits robbed our train and stole my wedding dress?"

Removing his hat, he squinted and brushed his hair. "Yes."

"All my letters blew out the window as well."

Christopher blinked. "Okay."

She thought he'd be more disappointed. Clearly, he crafted his letters with much care and attention. How was he not as heartbroken as she? "Well, I just wanted you to repeat some of the things you wrote in those letters, you know, as an assurance."

He narrowed his eyes. His whole body went rigid. "Are you regretting coming to Wylder?"

She grasped his arm. The wool of his calvary jacket warmed to her touch. Why was he so pale? "No, no! I just wanted to hear them again. I fell in love with the man who wrote those letters."

"You fell in love with the man who wrote those letters?" He shook her fingers from him and stood. The color drained from his face.

"Yes. I just need to hear you say those words." *Then all my fears will cease*, she didn't want to say.

"Listen." He bit his lip and patted her shoulder. "When I wrote those letters, I was a different person. In order to repeat those things, I'd have to become that person again, and I can't do that while I'm also thinking about protecting the town, you know?"

"Oh, sure. I understand." She slumped her shoulders. A sinking feeling swallowed her.

"I'll tell you what." He placed a gloved hand over her hand. "Tonight at the dance, I will share some of what was in those letters."

A balm eased her ache. "Thank you. I am looking forward to the wedding tomorrow."

He grinned wide. "Me, too. I have to go now. Duty

calls. I will see you at the dance."

She stood. The dance. All her fears would be assuaged at the dance tonight. She inhaled. She just had hesitations, right?

Chapter 12

Sitting at his work bench, Cyrus completed the finishing touches on Miss Maisie's six-shooter. So much of his heart went into designing this piece, from the choosing of the steel, to organizing and constructing it to the mother-of-pearl handles. In the end, when completed, he always engraved his cursive C into the underside of the grips, but he hesitated. The cursive C was the same mark he wrote on the bottom of his letters. If she saw it, she would know. Part of him wanted her to know, but then where would that leave Christopher? Cyrus couldn't crush the trust of his friendship. If only Christopher would confess, or if she asked or discovered the secret on her own, then he'd be free to confess his love but not before.

This piece represented his best work. He picked up the engraver and made his mark. He planned on giving it to her as an early wedding present today at the Independence Day celebration. He wasn't sure if he wanted to go to the wedding on Saturday. Watching her marry Christopher might make him sick.

Dancing with her was the closest thing to heaven he'd experienced. He still felt the warmth of her touch on his hand. The door bust open. Christopher filled the doorway, nearly blocking any light that would've come through.

Removing his hat, he widened his eyes. "We got

trouble."

Cyrus placed the small gun behind another piece and covered it with his design paper. "What happened?"

"Maisie wants me to tell her what was in the letters." Christopher paced. "Apparently, they were lost out the window or something." He scowled.

Dropping his tool, Cyrus froze. "What did you tell her?"

"I said I would let her know tonight. What are we going to do?"

"Don't panic." Cyrus stood then paced his shop and rubbed his unshaven chin. "We'll have to think of a way to relay the information. You can't read it from your hat. Likely, the school won't be lit enough to read."

"Wait." He held up his hand. "Are you saying you remember what you wrote in those letters?"

Cyrus rubbed his chin. "Of course I remember. But how to get you the information, that's the question." How dark would it be? He could wear Christopher's hat again, but if they were up close, she'd know right away. He'd have to cover his face. "I've got it. I will pretend to be you. I will wear your uniform and cover my face."

Christopher crossed his arms. "Won't she think it's a little suspicious if I come with a face covering?"

Christopher sounded rather put out. What had gotten into his friend? "I can say I have a cold. Or the dust bothers my nose."

"Maisie's a smart girl. I don't think she'd fall for it. Besides, she'll want to dance with you as well." A deep crease appeared in his forehead.

Cyrus raised his eyebrows. Would she? The

thought thrilled him.

"And I've invited the other soldiers to ask her as well."

Inhaling, Cyrus frowned. "I'll tell you what. I'll write down a few thoughts, you can read them over her shoulder while you dance. She won't see a thing."

Christopher grinned. "You really are the best friend. I was thinking, do you want to be my best man or give Maisie away?"

Energy drained from Cyrus. How could he give her away? Just being near her was the greatest of temptations. "I'll let you know tomorrow."

"I'll leave you so you can write up the words." Christopher opened the door. He paused by the wood frame. "She is in love with me, Cyrus. Maisie kissed me. She wants me." He stuck on his hat and strode out.

With face beating as hot as tempered steel, Cyrus stared at the mother-of-pearl handle. His heart ached. He couldn't wait for Saturday night to get here so he wouldn't have to keep torturing himself. He wrapped the gun in paper, tied a bit of string around it, locked the door, and went to find Maisie.

Even in her simple dress, she stood out from the crowd. Cyrus was awestruck by her beauty each time he saw her. Her bonnet hid her dark hair except for a ringlet or two around her neck. But her heart belonged to another. She and Cara walked the boards around the general store when he finally caught up to them.

"Miss Maisie." He removed his hat. "I have something for you."

She turned.

Her smile made his heart sing. The gloom and doom of all his self-doubt was swept away by her radiant smile.

"What is it?"

He handed her the package.

Her eyes lit up. She untied the string. Holding the gun in her gloved hands, she let out a little gasp. "I had no idea guns could be so beautiful. Thank you."

His heart rate picked up. "And I'm almost done with the flintlock, too. Got the hammer this morning, and I just need to find time to work on it."

After running a finger over the handle, she slipped the gun into her reticule. "You are too good. Please, let me know how much for the musket."

"No charge." And he meant it. "What have you ladies been out doing today?"

Maisie flashed a wide smile. "After we watched the pie contest, we witnessed the winner of the preserves receive her blue ribbon and clapped the small parade of veterans. Cara bought something from a vendor which the salesman promised to give her a glowing complexion."

He turned. Her face deepened to a nice pink. "I always thought your complexion a fine one, Miss Cara. No need to buy any fancy elixir. It is surely the color of buttermilk."

Lowering her chin, Cara blushed to the tips of her ears. "He promised my freckles would disappear."

Miss Maisie swung her dress from her hips. "She wants to look her best for the celebration tonight. Cara has a beau."

Cara's blush darkened and spread to her neck.

He raised his hat. "Well, I hope you will have a conquest tonight. But I request you'll both save me a dance."

"Oh, look. Christopher is at the shooting range." Cara pointed north of the sheriff's office. Against purple hills, Sheriff Wylder set up several poles with a paper target.

Cyrus slumped his shoulders. Christopher was the last person he wanted to see.

Maisie stepped forward and placed a hand on his forearm. "Let's go. I can try out my new gun. You can show me how to use it."

Energy flashed through Cyrus. Miss Maisie wanted a demonstration from him? "Sure, I can show you." Cyrus escorted the two ladies over to the shooting range with one woman on each arm. A fluttering sensation went through him.

Christopher held up his military-issued Springfield M 1873 breechloader rifle next to his cheek.

Cyrus never liked the copper .45 caliber rifle cartridges used in those things. In his shop, he'd extracted his fair share of jammed cartridges with a knife. When the bullets got stuck in the breech of the carbine in the heat of the moment, the gun could only be used as a poor hammer. "Mind if we join you?" Cyrus sidled next to the sheriff.

Christopher turned pink when he saw Miss Maisie. He grinned and nodded. He lowered his rifle.

Cyrus pointed toward the range. "Miss Maisie wanted to learn how to use her gun. You don't mind if we try it out while you're shooting, do you?"

"Sure." Christopher held up his breechloader to his cheek again. "I'm just practicing before I compete."

Why was Christopher being so awkward and cold? Cyrus squinted at his friend.

"You can use the range all you want, but if you

want to compete for Maybelle"—the young sheriff nodded to a red-headed heifer tied to a stake—"you'll have to pay."

Christopher lifted his rifle.

"Want to try your new gun?" Nodding toward Miss Maisie, Cyrus loaded a few bullets into her chambers. He always kept brass handy in the bandolier around his waist. He handed her the gun.

She blinked. "It's heavier than I would've expected."

"Slide your finger through the ring there, but don't squeeze the trigger just yet. Hold it steady." With a glance toward Christopher, Cyrus wrapped an arm around her and leaned close to her ear. "Close one eye. Now line up the rear sight and the front sight. Put your target in the center."

She adjusted her hand slightly and squished shut her eye.

"Now squeeze the trigger," Cyrus whispered.

The shot rang out.

Miss Maisie opened her other eye and lowered the gun. "That was incredible! And not nearly as scary as shooting the flintlock."

"Easy, right?" Cyrus ran his hands across her shoulders. Then he retracted his hands as if he'd been bit by a rattler. He was becoming too familiar. "Well done!"

Sheriff Wylder hooked his thumbs in his pockets. "And not a bad shot either." He grinned.

Christopher lowered his rifle. He rolled out his neck and thrust out his chest. "I was the rifle-shooting champion in our division's last competition. I'm gonna take this. Would you like that little heifer for our new home, Maisie?"

"What qualifies as a win?" Coughing, Cyrus squinted.

Miss Maisie focused on her gun.

The sheriff squinted at the poles. "Shoot all six poles with perfect bull's-eyes for the heifer. But I'll need a dollar to participate." He thumbed his pockets. "So far, more than fifty men have tried. No one has hit all six yet."

After digging into his pocket, Cyrus paid the sheriff. "I'm in."

"Don't you want to practice?" The sheriff cleared his throat.

"No need." Cyrus picked up the Mountie-model '76 Winchester Centennial lying on a blanket. He loaded the gun and pocketed the remaining brass. Then he rested the butt of the gun on his hip, the barrel pointing to the sky.

Christopher shot first, loading and shooting with precision. After he finished his six shots, he lowered his gun.

The sheriff strode out on the range to inspect. "Close, but the last one is a little off center. Let's see what skill Cyrus has."

Once Sheriff Wylder cleared the range, Cyrus brought up the Winchester to his cheek. He swallowed hard.

Miss Maisie stood to his left, holding her ears with gloved hands. She smiled and nodded.

Cyrus shot. He reloaded and shot again until all six were done. He didn't need the sheriff to confirm. He knew he hit them all bull's-eye. He lowered the Winchester and returned it.

"Well, I'll be…" The sheriff tucked his thumbs into his pockets. "All six. Clean bull's-eyes. Little Maybelle is yours."

Miss Maisie and Cara clapped.

"She'll be great on my little homestead." Pride burst through him. But he already got his reward. Seeing Miss Maisie cheer for him was worth more than a hundred head of cattle.

The sheriff nodded to a man holding the cow by a rope. "Frank can take her out to your place. And Captain Peele, you can pick from our basket of consolation prizes."

With downturned lips, Christopher stalked to the basket. He pulled out an emerald paste ring. "My dear, Maisie. I don't believe I have given you a token of my love." He slipped the gaudy thing over her gloved finger. The green flashed in the sun. Then, he swept her up into his arms and kissed her. He stepped away. "Shall we go see the exhibits?" He held out his arm. "Maisie?"

With flushed cheeks, she wiped her mouth, visibly caught off guard by the kiss. She glanced to her ring and toward Cyrus.

Cyrus's stomach heaved. He might have won the competition, but he lost the war.

****

The ring weighed on Maisie's finger, and her breath was still taken by Captain Peele's kiss. "Are you coming, too, Mr. Haddock?"

"I should return to the shop." He pointed behind his shoulder.

"Let's go look, shall we?" Doffing his hat and setting it back on his brow, Christopher headed toward the livestock.

"We'll all go." Skipping down the street, Cara grinned at Captain Peele. "This holiday only comes once a year. Let's look at the livestock. I've never seen anythin' so big as that bull." Holding on to her hat, Cara trailed after him. Her two silk ribbons flapped against her neck in the breeze. She followed him down Wylder Street around Backstreet to the corrals.

Maisie watched after them.

"Why do you hang back, Miss Maisie?" Cyrus walked beside her.

She inhaled. She didn't dare tell him all her thoughts. "I was just thinking of when I attended the World's Fair three years ago celebrating the one-hundredth anniversary of our nation in Philly. You would love it."

"I heard about it. They introduced the Seventy-Six Centennial Winchester there." He raised his hat to the sheriff and headed toward town.

Following, she grinned. Of course he knew about the guns. "The celebration was so different from this one. Thousands of people came every day to look at all the inventions. And the food! At the exposition, I ate something called popcorn. Do you know what that is?"

With an amused smile, he shook his head.

"They take dried corn and fry it in oil. Instead of a pan of grits, each kernel pops up white and fluffy! And they had this drink called root beer. I liked the taste, but a gentleman from France said it tasted like medicine." She laughed. Boston and her life seemed so far away and so different from now.

"Do you miss Boston?"

She kicked a pebble. Did people around them

wonder why she walked alone with a man? Maybe they did. She didn't care. "Sometimes. Everyone in Boston was defined by society. You either worked for money, or your money worked for you. Nothing in between. And the upper-class became very snooty. A hundred years ago we fought for the idea that all men were created equal, and yet some people set themselves above others. Boston grew stale. Here in the Wyoming Territory, the opportunities to make something of yourself—to define yourself—are still fresh. Someone once said that Wyoming Territory was for the dreamers, the creators, and the visionaries."

Cyrus grinned. "It is indeed. And you want to find what you can contribute."

Maisie bowed her head. Cyrus read her soul so completely. Despite only knowing him a few days, she was often shocked by how well he knew her. She focused on the ground, unsure what her heart meant.

"Looks like Cara and Christopher are getting on well."

Maisie raised her head to Cyrus, then followed his gaze toward the corrals. A horned beast pawed on strewn hay.

Christopher lifted up Cara so she could see the bull over the top of the fence.

She reached inside the fence to pet the bull.

When the bull snorted, both laughed. Cara exchanged glances and smiles with Captain Peele.

Maisie scowled. She'd seen that look before—between Harold Peabody and his maid. Her heart clenched. Not again.

"I'm sorry. I hope my observation didn't hurt you. Come. Let us join them."

Cyrus must've picked up on her frown. Despite everything, she had to marry Captain Peele. She would never go back to Boston and face her mother, and she couldn't support herself out here. A harrowing feeling haunted her as she crossed to the bullpen. What if Captain Peele found her repulsive? What if he changed his mind? He acted awfully cold at the shooting range.

"How's the bull?" Cyrus stuck his head over the fence.

"I once roped a bull." Captain Peele grinned at Maisie.

"Ye did?" Cara slapped him on the arm. "Tell me all about it."

Focusing on Cara, Captain Peele licked his lips. "Someone let loose a bunch of cattle, and they ran through town. Of course, we were called out to round up them all. This one gigantic bull snorted and pawed the ground, and he did not want to return to his pen."

Cara widened her eyes. "What did ye do?"

Captain Peele held out his hand, mimicking the action of a rope. "I used my trusty lariat and chased him down Copper Alley toward Bone Orchard Lane. He headed to the cemetery, but I couldn't allow him to trample those graves. So I galloped alongside him and roped his neck and dragged him back to the stock yards."

"How heroic!" Clapping her hands, Cara batted her blonde eyelashes and grinned.

Captain Peele retuned her smile.

Maisie's stomach roiled. "So heroic," she murmured.

Dropping her gaze, Cara glanced to Maisie. "Ye two will make a fine couple. Maisie wants to do something heroic."

Captain Peele shifted his gaze to Maisie. He smiled. "Does she now?"

Maisie blushed. How dare Cara mention that in public! Besides, Captain Peele should've known that from the letters. Sometimes he acted as if he hadn't read them. She flicked her gaze toward Cyrus. Did he think the secrets of her heart stupid?

He looked away.

Clasping the railing of the pen, Maisie cleared her throat. "I just want to make something of my life—something worthy of being in the newspaper."

Captain Peele grabbed her around the shoulders. "You can be in the newspaper for having the most children in Wylder." He whooped.

Gulping, Maisie forced a grin. A sinking feeling filled her stomach.

Throwing back her head and laughing, Cara clapped her hands. "What a grand notion!"

A wave of nausea washed over her. Maisie must've gotten overheated.

"Perhaps we can see more exhibits up here." Cyrus nodded with his head toward the other side of Wylder Street. "I want to buy something to eat. Maisie told me about some food she ate at a fair, and that sounds tasty right about now. Anyone else hungry?"

Cara started off. "Oh, yes, food sounds mighty fine. What are ye hungry for, Captain Peele?"

"I could eat a horse." With a guffaw, he followed her.

Maisie remained behind. "Thank you," she said to Cyrus.

"You looked a little unwell." He walked slowly.

Standing on his good side, Maisie kept pace. "Indeed, I felt ill." She paused. Her illness had nothing to do with hunger. "I—"

Cyrus pitched his eyebrows. "Cara is full of enthusiasm."

Maisie sighed. Thankfully, he turned the subject to Cara. She might've told Cyrus how little their flirtations pained her. "She lived a small life as a maid. Everything here is new. She's easily excited."

"The dance tonight will be an event for her."

Nodding, Maisie studied the backs of both Christopher and Cara. "This dance will be her first. I dare say she will be thrilled with the attention. From all the men." Dread grew in Maisie's stomach, but she couldn't pinpoint exactly what it was. All she knew was her wedding couldn't come soon enough. Once she was married, she was sure this terrible feeling would go away.

****

"Fourth of July." Gambell grinned as his horse clopped into Wylder again Friday evening. Like many a town out West, this one was no different. Buildings— some brick like the bank; some clapboard, like the saloon—stood along dirt roads and rose out of the sagebrush. Planks lined the roadside like the vertebrae of a snake. A few establishments had small shelters over the doorways. Others contained large windows imported from back East. The train tracks ran east to west in the middle of town next to the old stagecoach stop and the Wells Fargo office.

He'd forgotten about the holiday. While living on the lam since he deserted the army, he rarely marked the days with any particular notice. What did he care for the birth of a country who actively hunted him for the bounty on his head for deserting an army fighting for a cause he cared little for? He wasn't a coward. He just didn't want to die in a pointless war. Now he needed to clear his name so he could marry the love of his life, Darlene. But first he had to settle a score or two.

Someone in town set out tables covered with blankets for preserves, quilts, and pies. If he were lucky, any killing would be swallowed up in the sound of fireworks, dances, and commotion planned for tonight according to a posted sign. But he had to wait. The sun hadn't set. He and his friends should spend a little time at the saloon until then, getting a drink to stiffen their courage. The drink never failed him.

First things first. "Johnson, Barclay!" His trusted friends were always at his side. "Scout the town and find where this woman lives. She came into town on Tuesday with the train. Someone will know where she lives."

The two led their horses to the hitching posts near the festivities.

Barclay slouched off his horse. "Sure thing, Gambell."

Johnson scratched the growth on his chin. "Why do we have to do the investigating?"

Johnson had a big mouth and always shouted. Gambell rolled his eyes. "Because I'm the one the woman has seen. Just spread out and ask questions. Judging by her wedding gown, I bet the dress shop lady knows where she lives. Barclay, see if the dressmaker's shop is open."

Barclay nodded and sauntered up the road.

"I still don't like it." Johnson kicked a rock and stuck his thumbs in his gun belt, then headed after Barclay.

Douglas and Strubb remained. Strubb needed a bath something awful—like garlic left in the sun too long. Gambell shifted so he wasn't downwind.

Douglas followed suit. "What do we do now?"

Gambell grinned and studied the scene of merriment before him. "We'll lay low until the nighttime."

A half-hour later, Barclay returned, shuffling down the street. "Dressmaker wasn't in the shop; however, she was outside. Turns out she is quite a talker and has no fondness for the new lady in town. A Maisie Brinley is living at Culpepper's Boarding House up yonder."

"Perfect." Gambell gripped the reins with his good arm. "I'd like to settle the score."

Chapter 13

Darkness fell on Wylder. Someone lit hundreds of candles in the school room, and they twinkled like the endless Wyoming sky. Maisie couldn't wait to go to her room and prepare for the dance.

Cara returned already to get dressed in Maisie's peach silk dress.

But Maisie lingered on Wylder Street. The thousands of lights almost made the schoolhouse glow as bright as day. Inside, women decorated and set up food tables. Anticipation hung in the air.

The evening air brought a fresh, cool breeze filled with the scent of sagebrush. Couples, linked arm in arm, headed toward the schoolhouse. A fiddle tuned and warmed up.

As she strolled toward the boardinghouse, Maisie wondered what the night would bring. Perhaps Christopher would suddenly come to his senses, and she would rekindle her love. With a trill of excitement, she mounted the inside stairs.

Eulalia Culpepper sailed into the parlor.

"Are you going to the dance tonight?" Maisie lifted her skirts to take the next step.

"Why would I want to see a bunch of people wasting time?" Eulalia lowered her brows.

"Well, have a good night then." Maisie reached the room and opened the door.

Cara, still in her day clothes, was face down on the bed, crying.

"What happened?" Maisie rushed to her side and sat on the squeaking bed. She touched Cara's trembling shoulder.

"Go away!"

"What's wrong? Did something happen?"

"I canno' go to the dance tonight." Her voice was muffled through the blankets.

"Why not?"

Cara lifted her head.

Gasping, Maisie widened her eyes. Cara's sweet complexion, usually fair, was now red and peeling.

She swore by the holy family. "Oh, that *while* man promised to remove me freckles. The stuff is burnin' off me *bake*! Now I'll miss all the *craic*."

Maisie couldn't understand her slang, but she could understand her heartache. "Let's get some cool water on it." She poured water into the bowl, dipped in the cotton towel, and brought it to Cara's blotchy face. "That must be painful."

"It hurts like Satan's hellfire." Tears fell over her blistered cheeks and onto the patchwork quilt. "I canno' go to the dance."

"Oh, my heart." The bed squeaked under Maisie as she moved to care for her friend's face. "I will stay with you. You poor thing." She patted the red spots gently with her towel.

Cara sniffed. "Nonsense. Ye should go without me."

"I won't." Although she'd be disappointed not to dance with Captain Peele or Cyrus. She persuaded Cyrus to come. If she didn't show, she wouldn't be honorable. What would Cyrus think of her?

Cara's lip trembled. "Ye must go, or ye'll disappoint the captain."

Oh, yes, the captain. She was engaged to *him*. "He'll understand if I don't make it."

"This is yer last day before ye wed. Ye must go to the dance." She laid down her head, then picked it up. "And ye can wear the peach silk dress since I will no' be able to."

"I'm fine wearing this simple dress."

Huge tears spilled on her reddened cheeks. "Ach, me vanity is punishin' me. I coveted yer silk dress, and this is where vanity led me. Me mother says covetin' is a sin. And I coveted yer fine skin. Ye have no freckles, ye see. And I covet—"

Maisie placed a hand over Cara's mouth. "Hush now. The peach silk is yours. I will wear this." She pinched her skirt. "No use lamenting or confessing. I promise you'll attend other dances." Maisie stroked her red hair and kissed the top of her head.

"Ye better go. The dance—the music started."

Violin strains floated on the night's breeze through the open window.

After one last hug, Maisie slipped out. Once in the hall, she leaned against the wall, exhaling. At least Cara wouldn't be throwing herself at Captain Peele all night, and Maisie would right her own feelings. Lifting her hem, she scampered downstairs. With a cheerful goodnight to Mrs. Culpepper, she dashed out the door to the schoolhouse. Fiddle music rang throughout the streets. The notes sent a thrill of excitement through her heart.

Cyrus stood outside near the wooden entrance. He

shaved and changed his clothes from earlier. When he spotted her, he smiled. His fingers clasped a bouquet of tiny blue and magenta buds. "I thought you might appreciate a nosegay of wildflowers."

She accepted the posies in an intricately engraved small, silver cone no bigger than her thumb. "It's beautiful." Heat overtook her. She plucked the miniature flowers and sniffed rays of sunshine and earth. "Thank you. Did you make this tussy mussy?"

A tint of pink colored his neck and matched the red of the scarred side of his face. "I was going to save it for your wedding…"

"Will you pin it on me?" She gulped at her boldness. Leaning closer, he delicately pinched a bit of fabric at her collarbone with his warm hands and slid the pin through, then set the clasp. He smelled of rosemary soap and shaving tonic. She held her breath. His nearness sent shivers clear to her stockinged toes.

Stepping back, his gaze shone in the darkness. "You promised me one dance tonight, Miss Maisie."

"Just one?" She looked forward to monitoring his dancing progress, or perhaps she anticipated his arms around her again.

He smiled clear to his eyes. "At least one."

Fiddle strains blew from the open doors of the schoolhouse. Maisie tapped her boots. A cough sounded behind her. She spun.

With slicked back hair, Captain Peele in his military blues grinned, hat tucked under his arm. He stuck out his gloved hand. "The music's playing. We should get on the dance floor."

Maisie glanced over her shoulder to catch Cyrus's reaction, but he'd disappeared amongst the crowd of people entering the school. She furrowed her brow. She'd have to catch him later for a dance.

Captain Peele led the way across the puncheon floor.

She nearly stumbled on the unevenness of the rough hewn boards beneath her feet. Her slippers would get a pounding tonight.

Men outnumbered the women more than two to one. Sheriff Wylder stood at the front, checking cavalry swords from the government employees, guns from townsfolk, and spurs from men returning from the range. A dozen men still wore work clothes from the day, but the casual attire didn't spoil the fun.

All the children's desks were moved elsewhere. A table spread with prizewinning pies sat along one wall, ribbons attached to each pie tin. At the end, a fine pewter punchbowl swirled with promising refreshment. Thousands of candles and lamps lined the rafters above them and dripped wax on shoulders at intervals. The room smelled of smoke, leather, and dust.

A band clustered at one end. The fiddler tuned the instruments and led the tempo with his bow before joining in sharp strains.

The first tune was a lancer's dance she knew well. The uneven floor made the gliding movements more difficult than the polished floors in Boston. More than once, she tripped into Captain Peele's arms. How Cara would've loved to be here, dancing. So many men needed a partner. The crush of people made it nearly impossible to breathe. While completing a turn, she glimpsed Cyrus standing in a corner with his hip cocked, leaning against the wall, watching her. A flutter shuddered through her.

Conversation with the Captain seemed impossible over the bustle and separation of the dance. She was not within earshot for more than a few seconds before the next set of movements. The Captain mostly just stared anyhow.

"Are you excited for tomorrow?" When they were together, he leaned forward to yell over the music.

"Yes." Now she separated. An emotion flashed in her stomach. She supposed it could be nerves or excitement. A wry smile passed on her lips.

Back together, he raised his chin. "I've been thinking we can buy a little homestead out of town."

"Sounds nice." She hopped to her companion at her left. This was the first time he'd talked specifics. Her stomach turned.

Together again, he held her hand. "Raise a couple of head of cattle, a herd of goats, and maybe a dozen chickens."

His dream sounded nice but distant. "Tell me the promises you wrote in your letters."

Captain Peele gulped and shot away a glance. "I can't concentrate on those things now—not with the music and the people."

She nodded. Maisie longed to connect her heart and soul to the heart and soul of the man in the letters. The connection was a chord. One she could almost reach out and pluck. Yet Captain Peele constantly dismissed his feelings and never discussed anything he wrote. She yearned for those conversations.

The music ended. Pinching her skirts at the sides, she curtsied low.

Captain Peele tugged at his high collar. "My, it's dry in here. It's a wonder they haven't set this place ablaze with all this candlelight. I'm getting myself a glass of liquid refreshment." He dashed off in the direction of the punch bowl.

Left alone on the dance floor, Maisie wasn't sure what to do. Swirling in her skirt, she dodged the next set of couples as they readied for the next dance. Unsure if Christopher would rejoin her or not, she waded through arms and chests to get to the wall. From behind, someone tugged on her arm.

Through the forest of bodies, Cyrus found her. His eyes danced. "I thought he'd never leave you." He raised his eyebrows. "Dance with me?"

"I'd love to." A burst of excitement zinged through her.

The music slowed to a waltz. Her mother hated the waltz. She could hear her voice in her head. "Dancing closed-off from all other contact is indecent." At any other time, Maisie would've found the waltz terribly dull and boring, preferring the more active dances, but this time she relished the time with Cyrus.

Expertly, Cyrus slid his hand over her back at her waist and took her hand in his. The touch thrilled her. She almost gasped for breath. He spun her effortlessly around the floor. His usual musk of smoke and black powder was gone, replaced with a homey scent of soap.

Her eyes narrowed. He danced a little too skillfully. "You do know how to dance."

A raw chuckle emerged from his throat. "We had to learn in the military. Even non-commissioned officers were required to attend military balls."

She gave him a little punch on the shoulder. "You tricked me."

He shook his head. "I never said I couldn't dance.

Only that I needed lessons."

"Deception." But she couldn't even feign anger. Her cheeks hurt, holding in a smile.

Tilting his head, he grinned. "I might've deceived you a little. Will you forgive me?"

She heaved an exaggerated sigh. "I suppose." A grin broke through her pretended harshness. She couldn't stay mad.

He held her close, closer than she'd ever been to a man except Christopher and Harold. At some points in the dance, his knees brushed against her thighs. A rush of heat filled her body. Her heartbeat thrummed in her ears. Darkness gathered at the edges of her eyes. She leaned close to his solid chest. He stared down through thickly-lashed eyes. His cool breath brushed against her face.

"You're flushed. You need some cool air."

"I think I do." She gulped.

The music hadn't ended, but he stopped and led her off the crowded dance floor to the open door to the side.

Immediately, cool air hit her cheeks. Away from the music and the heat and the crowd, her heart rate slowed. Her hem snagged on bushes. She wandered across the brush to a split rail fence near the edge of the property. The music faded. Only the sounds of the night echoed in her ears—mosquitoes buzzing, owls hooting, animals yipping. The vast blackness of the plains and hills stretched along the horizon. She inhaled the cooler air of hay, sage, and a hint of the wildflowers tucked in her shirt.

Sounds like gunshots echoed off the hills. Fireworks exploded in the air above the town. Flashes of light lit up Cyrus.

Chapter 14

Patting his chest holster for his gun, Cyrus swore under his breath. The sheriff made him check his piece before attending the dance. Thankfully, he carried a spare in his boot holster. He snatched up the single shooter and followed Maisie and a crowd of others across town to Culpepper's Boarding House. Creaking up the stairs, he entered the front parlor.

"Are they still in there?" someone asked behind him. People stood in the doorway. A lamp was still on inside. But the house was quiet.

Cyrus tiptoed around the first floor. Nothing seemed to be out of place.

Maisie followed.

Without waiting for the sheriff, he trudged up the steps. He waved Maisie back down the stairs.

She clung to his arm. "I'm coming with you."

The sheriff probably didn't take guns from the women. He nodded. "Stay behind me. Got your piece?"

"Right here." She held up the small six shooter she retrieved from her pocket.

Sweat prickled his skin. "Don't shoot at anything unless you clearly recognize it."

"My room is up there." She motioned with her head.

He nodded. He already knew where she stayed since he pretended to be Christopher her first night in

159

town. Listening for anything out of the ordinary, he crept up the tread slowly. He traced the outside of the house in his head. Her window was the third over so he needed to pass two doors. A sliver of light shone from the third room in the hall. "Your door is open."

"How did you know that's my door?"

Shoot! He gulped. "Lucky guess." As he approached the left-swing door, he halted near the right door jamb, inhaled, then jumped into the doorframe and slammed open the door.

Nobody was inside; however the room was spoiled. Sheets were stripped from the bed. Everything was removed from the trunks and was strewn about the floor. More than a few lacy underthings lay exposed. He blushed. The mirror over the vanity was shattered, as was the water pitcher and bowl for washing. The towel stand blocked the closet door at an angle. He waded through the room, careful not to disturb anything. "Is anything missing?" He glanced over his shoulder to Maisie, to avoid landing his gaze on anything too frilly.

"Where's Cara?" Maisie's eyes grew large.

Stepping gently around shards of broken porcelain, he threw open the closet door. Empty.

"Cara?" Maisie shouted. Throwing open the door, she entered the hall.

Her panicked voice continued down the hall.

"Cara, are you here?"

Biting his lip, Cyrus kicked the clothes, searching for any blood or signs of physical harm.

Maisie creaked open the door. "Mrs. Culpepper said they took her. There were six men. One tall man had yellow hair."

Her large blue eyes were as big as wagon wheels. Her face paled.

Gambell. Cyrus gulped. He shuddered at the idea of sweet Cara with those vagabonds. He set his jaw. "We'll find Cara. Six men will leave a trail. We can track them."

Maisie pointed toward the window. "But it's dark." She burst into tears.

"We'll start at first light."

Footfalls sounded on the stairs. The sheriff and others bustled into the hall. "What happened?"

Shaking his head, he motioned he'd speak in a minute. By taking her hand, Cyrus led Maisie out the door.

Christopher stood at the top of the stairs.

Maisie ran to Christopher and cried into his chest.

Stroking her hair, he swallowed her in a hug.

Gulping, Cyrus felt as if his heart was carved with a knife.

The sheriff buckled on his hip holster. "Will you tell me what's going on here?"

Cyrus pointed into the room. "Six men kidnapped a young woman. If we form a posse, we can track them and bring her back."

"Who is the girl?" Sheriff Wylder arched a brow.

Cyrus shook his head. "A friend who came with Miss Brinley."

"Why would they take a girl?" The sheriff squinted his eyes.

"I'm not risking my life for no Irish woman." A man in the back retreated and thundered down to the parlor.

Cyrus waited until Christopher escorted Maisie

downstairs. "This is the same band who robbed the train coming into Cheyenne and the gang who stole revolvers from my shop. Whoever brings them in could claim the bounty."

"Are you sure?" a redheaded man in the back asked.

"I'm sure." Cyrus nodded. "They targeted Miss Brinley for revenge. They kidnapped Cara to hurt Miss Brinley. Let us form a posse and—"

The sheriff pointed to the men surrounding the door. "Take whoever is willing to go with you. And you have the right of law. We'll leave at dawn."

Cyrus slapped the sheriff on his shoulders. "Thank you." Cyrus would like nothing more than to have his revenge on the men who terrorized his shop and Maisie. He thundered down the stairs.

Mrs. Culpepper sat on a couch. Her bun hung around her left ear. "They destroyed my room. Who will pay for all the damages?" With reddened eyes, Mrs. Culpepper pointed across the room to Maisie, still sobbing into a handkerchief. "She will. This mess is all her fault."

Christopher turned Maisie from a wailing Mrs. Culpepper, burying her in his chest.

Cyrus placed a hand on his empty hip holster where his gun usually sat and faced the weeping woman. "A woman has been kidnapped, Mrs. Culpepper. Her life is in danger. Don't worry about the damages. You'll be reimbursed. Right now, why don't you get Miss Brinley some tea? Her friend has been taken, and all you think about is money."

Blinking, Mrs. Culpepper widened her eyes.

Cyrus suspected she wasn't used to being spoken

to in such a harsh manner, but he had just enough of her complaining.

Then her eyes narrowed. In a huff, she sailed back into the kitchen.

Satisfied Mrs. Culpepper wouldn't be bothering Maisie again tonight, Cyrus replaced his hat and grabbed the front door handle, then turned to beckon Christopher.

Christopher embraced Maisie again. He bent and kissed her. "They'll be asking for men to track the kidnappers. They couldn't have gone far. I'll be heading out with them."

Maisie's shoulders shook. "Bring her home safe. Please."

"I'm honor bound to return Cara." He lifted Maisie's chin. "Although, my leaving will likely postpone our wedding for tomorrow night."

Widening her eyes, Maisie sniffed. She shook her head, curls dancing around her forehead. "Wedding? Who can think of marriage when Cara is in danger?"

Relaxing, Cyrus exhaled, releasing the door handle. The wedding was postponed.

"You will be my champion and bring her home." She kissed Christopher one more time.

The kiss must've filled him with energy, for after they parted, Christopher threw on his hat, bolted for the door, and yipped into the night. "We'll be back in no time with Cara."

With a burning chest, Cyrus lowered his gaze to the floor boards and ragged carpet in Mrs. Culpepper's dingy parlor. He had no proclamations to make, no oaths, and no promises. Turning to leave, he replaced his hat.

Maisie snatched his elbow. "Bring him home safely to me. I love him so much."

Bile turned in his stomach. His heart felt about to burst. "I promise no harm will come to Christopher." Even if his life meant nothing to her, he would gladly lay it down. She captured his heart, his soul, and his mind. He was powerless against any request she might ask. "If we are both to leave, you must protect yourself. Come with me." He led the way out the door.

The air turned rather chilly. His breath curled in steamy tendrils against the moonlight, turning on Buckboard Alley toward his shop. Remembering to leave open the door when he entered, he unlocked his shop, lit the oil lamp, and found the flintlock. "Here." He handed her the piece. "It's ready. You have this flintlock and the handgun. Remember, you only need about a teaspoon of powder, not a teacup." He grinned and placed the muzzleloader into her hands.

She trembled. "I don't really know how to use this as evidenced by the fact I blew up the whole mechanism last time."

"Hold the gun here." Wrapping his arms around her, he placed the gun in the crook of her arm. The nearness made him dizzy. "Align this notch with that one to give you a clear shot, like the revolver. Do you see it?"

"Yes."

He was nearly cheek to cheek with her. The smell of her hair intoxicated him. His heart ached to part with her. "If you can keep your target within your sights, you won't miss." He stepped away. Coldness swept into the space between them.

She lowered the gun.

Unable to stand her beauty and goodness all at once, he turned. Returning his attention to packing, he picked up a few guns and extra ammo.

"I will miss our talks," she murmured.

He didn't dare look up. If he did, he might confess all. Instead, he busied himself with gathering irons. So much burdened his heart.

She slipped out the door.

Standing at the door, he watched her return home. He stilled his breath. He only had to make it through until the two were wed. Christopher would safely return and would marry Maisie. Yet, where did that leave his heart? He decided to leave one last letter. He sat at his bench, drew out paper and pen, and wrote the thoughts of his heart.

Chapter 15

Cyrus scowled at the clouds muddying the dawn and threatening rain. A light drizzle in the early morning softened the ground, making the tracks easier to find. But any harder rain and they'd wash away.

Near town, the kidnappers' hoof prints were sparse and deep—easy to track. The rowdies travelled west, fast across the terrain. Now inside Colorado, the kidnappers slowed their mounts. They were probably confident no one followed them. The tracking slowed as the weather deteriorated and water flooded the ground. Rain, coming in torrents, washed away any sign of travelers.

By midmorning, the party split, and the sheriff led half a dozen men straight north in case the outlaws decided to flee into Canada.

On the horse next to Cyrus, Christopher largely kept silent the whole trip. Was the bad weather quieting him, or was he worried about Cara or Maisie? His blue uniform was soaked through.

At least Cyrus's hat kept the drops out of his face, but the rainfall lashed his McCoy waxed duster he pinched from a fallen Confederate officer in the war. When the rain came too hard, he nodded toward a grove. They needed to stop. "You men shelter in those cottonwoods." He wanted to examine the ground again. The terrain turned rockier, but he hoped for signs along the creek where the ground was softer. The streams swelled from the rain. Crossing was no problem on horseback. If he couldn't find tracks, he'd have to head into the bush looking for broken twigs and disturbed branches. Searching for small clues would slow them down.

Dismounting Salt and Pepper, he nodded a wordless thanks to his five companions. He'd been disappointed at the turnout for the ride. Besides him and Christopher, only four other men—good men—remained. If they found the roughs, six against six weren't the odds he hoped for, but less than a dozen men wanted to risk their lives for a little Irish girl who'd only been in town a few days. Cyrus couldn't blame them.

Adjusting his hat, he stepped carefully into a cluster of sagebrush. His experience tracking and recognizing signs of disturbances led the posse this far. Even an overturned rock or leaf could be the tip he needed.

Christopher followed into the bush.

Cyrus pointed west with his head. "Across this creek here is the Virginia Dale Overland station. It's been abandoned for about ten years now. If they are tired or hungry, they might wait out the rain there." Cyrus wanted to catch them as quickly as possible yet his stomach turned at the thought of returning to Christopher and Maisie's wedding. "A homestead is just south of here. They might seek shelter there as well." He studied a few broken branches.

A few horse hoof prints marked the rocky soil. His heartbeat kicked up. Signs!

Crouching, he picked up a fallen stick and pointed

to half-tracks. "If you look at the wall here, these are recent." He laid out two lengths of rope alongside the dominant footprint to calculate the direction. "My best guess is they went west, toward the station." He nodded in the general direction. "If we hurry, we can catch them." He wiped his hands free of rocky mud.

Nearby, Christopher wandered into the bush. "I learned how to track, too, in the US Army. Looking at this set of tracks, I'd guess they headed southwest, toward the homestead." With his boot, he drew two parallel lines going more southwest.

Placing his hands on his holster, Cyrus shook his head. He didn't want to argue. Cyrus was right. Christopher didn't have the experience he had. "I don't think your methods are precise."

Thrusting out his chest, Christopher narrowed his eyes. "Are you questioning an officer in the US Calvary?"

Cyrus shrugged. "I'm not sure your methods are accurate. What you did looked a little sloppy. You have to be precise when tracking men. You've never seen wartime combat..."

Christopher thrust out his chest. "Don't throw your military service into my face. I see things every day."

Christopher's disrespect bothered Cyrus. He didn't appreciate his terse voice. "Maybe you can track bison herds, but nothing is like tracking a man. Man is clever, resourceful, and deceitful."

"Let's ask the posse which way they think we should go." Christopher spun. When he reached the shaded grove, he addressed the men. "We have a choice. Cyrus thinks the tracks head west toward Virginia Dale station. I picked up a set of tracks heading southwest. Which ones do we want to take?"

Hanks and Jefferies glanced away.

What perturbed Christopher? He was never this snappish. Cyrus rubbed his chin. "Or we could split up and take them both."

Spitting tobacco, Hanks furrowed his rusted eyebrows. "Split up? Are you kidding me? If we encounter the roughs, we'd be outnumbered two to one."

Cyrus faced Hanks. "But if we head in the wrong direction, we could lose them. I say we head to the Dale. Or split and follow both trails."

Hanks raised his chin. "And I say your plan stinks. Just like you stink."

Cyrus didn't even bat an eye at the red-headed man. "I'm sorry if I don't bathe according to your schedule. Do you all feel this way?"

The three others kept their gazes on the ground.

Cyrus sighed. "Well, then fine. You can go toward the homestead. And I'll head to Virginia Dale." He picked up his reins and lifted his foot to the stirrup.

Hanks squinted. "And you're ugly. Your face looks like it was bit off by a coyote."

Heat flashed Cyrus. Energy poured through him. He threw down his reins and stepped closer, ready to tear Hanks from his saddle. "Bit off by a coyote? Is that all you've got in your pea brain? I've heard insults about my face that would scald the hair off a boar pig."

Christopher jumped between Cyrus and Hanks and held Cyrus's shoulders. "Calm down. No one needs to get shot today. Least of all Hanks."

Cyrus glared at the belligerent man, then headed toward his horse.

"Actually." Hanks rose into his saddle. "Me and Jefferies here are done. The rain washed out the tracks. We can't find them. While you guys were squabbling in the brush, we decided we're heading back."

Cyrus stared hard at Hanks. "Fine. Go home." Four to six was still a doable number. They could take the kidnappers. He went to Salt and Pepper.

Christopher mounted his horse. "We're going to the homestead. Looks like you're on your own."

He faced his friend. "What is wrong with you?"

Narrowing his eyes, Christopher gripped the reins on his horse, chomping at the bit. "You shouldn't even be on this trip, and yet you act like the leader."

Was that what irritated him? Christopher wanted to take charge? Cyrus rolled his eyes. Fine…let them go. He could sneak up on the kidnappers at Virginia Dale and catch them by surprise while the others followed a false trail. He faced his horse again.

"You're not going to be the hero."

Cyrus straightened his spine. What did he mean?

"You won't be the one to impress Maisie."

Cyrus froze. Exactly where his heart stood with Miss Maisie, he couldn't tell Christopher. "I just want my guns back." He grabbed the pommel.

Christopher jabbed a gloved finger. "You like her."

Heat rose under Cyrus's duster. Keeping his breathing steady, he stuck his leg into the stirrup and kicked his right leg over the horse. He settled himself in the saddle before answering. "Of course I like her. She's a nice lady." Cyrus's chest split in two at the lies.

Snarling, Christopher spat. "I see the way you stare at her—the way she smiles at you."

Flames burst within him. If only he could tell

Christopher about his feelings for Miss Maisie. "I don't know what you're imagining."

"Open your eyes, Cyrus. Are you blind as well as ugly?"

Cyrus reeled from the insult from his friend. If he hadn't promised his safety... "What do you mean?" He narrowed his eyes.

"I see you talking."

"So we converse." Despite his galloping heart choking his breath, Cyrus shrugged and gripped his reins. So Christopher's runaway imagination made him so testy these last few days?

Christopher scowled. "Yes, but it's the *way* you talk. Anyone can see it. You tell her things she cares about."

Cyrus's heart couldn't take any more of this. If he didn't leave soon, he'd do something he would later regret.

"Why are you the one she listens to?" Christopher curled his lip and shook his head.

Christopher's words lanced daggers into his heart. What was he getting at? Did he want Cyrus to admit his feelings? Cyrus wouldn't go there.

"All this time she's been mooning over those letters." Christopher lowered his voice and bent over his horse. "I'm going to make her love me for me." He whipped his horse and took off at a full gallop with the two men trailing him.

Cyrus sat back into the saddle. Heat flushed through him. He gripped his reins until his fists hurt. Christopher was a fool, but was Cyrus a bigger fool?

****

Maisie barely slept. Throughout the night, she

peered out the window. A man standing guard below in only a duster against the rain gave her small measure of peace. She brushed a hand over the cold spot on the bed beside her.

But what of Cara? Who watched over her? The thoughts haunted her dreams and terrified her in the day.

Late last night, Mrs. Culpepper exchanged the broken pitcher for a fresh one. But only a shard or two remained in the mirror frame. Maisie stared at herself in the fractured pieces.

Today was supposed to be her wedding day. Now instead, her groom searched for Cara—nightmares of nightmares. She heard the men leave at drizzly dawn with the sound of hoofbeats.

Even at nearly ten, the room was barely light. Clouds covered the usually cerulean sky and poured a fair measure of rain over Wylder. Maisie wished to spend all day in bed but knew she couldn't. She slid from the covers.

A paper folded in thirds sat on her floorboards just inside her door. Still in her nightdress, she bent and picked it up. She unfolded it.

A letter from Christopher. A jolt went through her. He hadn't forgotten her during his preparations for departure. Her heart melted. He hadn't so much as said goodbye, other than their embrace last night, and she was about ready to never forgive him for his neglect. This letter was a balm to all her unhappy feelings during the night.

Pulling up her night gown, she curled in bed, turned up the oil, lamp, and caressed the ink.

5 July 1879

My Dearest Maisie,

My thoughts are harried on this night of all nights when I am forced to leave you, my dear. You cannot imagine the ache that hollows my chest. You, alone, are in my thoughts. With every preparation, your voice echoes in the chambers of my heart. With every bullet I load, I think, I go to avenge you, my love.

I have not rested since you stepped foot into Wylder. You are a flood, whisking away every piece of me. When you are near, I tremble. When we part, I think of our shared words. They are manna to my soul. Every thought of you is a drink in a desert. I go tonight with thoughts of you on my lips and eagerly anticipate my return so that I can hold you in my arms again. Your love has given me courage; you are an elixir of vigor and power. Your confidence gives me strength beyond ten men. If asked, I could forge the Mississippi River. With your love, I can cross a continent. You have created a monster, a Frankenstein—for my heart is yours, my mind is yours, and my body is yours to command. I am no longer master of my fate. I do as you demand.

If you ask it, I would lay down my life. If you commanded, I would raise it up again. As you require, I protect others with my life.

Your willing servant,

C

With a thundering heart, she clasped the letter to her heart and sighed. Then she reread a portion that gave her pause. Christopher truly thought of their discussions? How odd. She couldn't remember having any significant conversations. She shrugged. Even the smallest words have the biggest impact.

She caressed the cursive *C* at the bottom of the letter and kissed it. The mark meant so much. Every letter with this mark sent rays of sunshine into her heart. The *C* was the bearer of good news and heightened feeling. If only they could send letters after they were married. She clung to his letters—the only glue left in their relationship.

Maisie tilted her head. She'd seen the mark somewhere else, but she couldn't remember where. Maybe she'd seen it on something of Christopher's.

Outside, rain fell in a terrible downpour. Likely she wouldn't be going out this morning. But she should at least dress and carry on some semblance of normalcy. She poured water and washed then dressed herself. With every loop of her corset, she thought of Cara. Perhaps someone in town had news already.

The rain slowed to a drizzle, and she hooked her boots and headed downstairs. Without saying good day to Mrs. Culpepper, she stepped out into the damp afternoon. A general buzz around the sheriff's office drew her attention. Maisie stopped a passerby. "What's going on?"

"Hanks and Jefferies returned. They said the tracks were all washed out. After the sheriff headed north, the posse split into two groups Cyrus went one way, and Christopher took two more the other way."

Her heart froze. "They left them? They will need more men. Will anyone else go?" She stared into the faces of the surrounding men.

Many cast down their gazes.

A red-headed man she thought named Hanks spit tobacco in the mud. A trail of dark juice ran down his lips. Maisie turned up her nose.

"Nobody wants to risk their life for no Irish girl."

Maisie's chest burned. She narrowed her eyes. "Fine. I will go myself."

Hanks squinted and pushed up his hat. "Beggin' your pardon, Miss Maisie. How will you get there?"

"I need a sidesaddle and a guide." She searched the faces of the men. The tobacco chewer looked shrewd.

"Where do you think you'll get one?" Crossing his arms across his chest, Hanks smirked. "Little Miss High-and-Mighty has found herself in a bind."

All her Boston upbringing and Mother's words filled her. She narrowed her eyes and readied to give him a tongue-lashing his grandchildren would remember. Then Cara's words echoed in her ears. *You'll win more friends with honey than vinegar.*

Being nice to such men was humiliating. Maisie bit her lip. Her money could buy their goods as she relied on in the past. Money was a language most people understood. Yet money couldn't buy their loyalty. And she needed a guide. She stamped her foot.

The men grinned. Some turned away.

She bit her tongue until it nearly bled. Could she sacrifice her pride to help Christopher and Cara? She gulped. "When I first came to this town, I thought you all unrefined and uncouth." She raised her voice so the small crowd of twenty or so could hear. "But in the last four days, I have seen something so much greater than refinement. I have seen resourcefulness, kindness, community, and acceptance. This sense of independence is something I haven't seen for a long time where I come from. I am proud to call Wylder home."

Sneers turned to smiles. Men nodded.

Honey *did* work better. Maisie couldn't believe how their expressions softened. She pointed to the tobacco-chewer. "You there. Hanks, is it? I've heard you are the most experienced around here. Would you be willing to take me back to where they split up?"

Hanks lifted his eyebrows. He spat again. His eyes softened a little at the compliment. "Depends on how much you're willing to pay."

"Fifty dollars." She brought four times as much here to use to start her home. Digging into her reticule, she found the bill and lifted it up. It crinkled between her fingers. "Issued from the Massachusetts Bank."

Men in the crowd raised their eyebrows. A few bystanders on the boards gasped. The Massachusetts Bank was one of the oldest in the country.

Grinning, Hanks slapped his thigh. "Shoot. For fifty cash, I'll take you back to where we left them. But then I won't go any farther."

"You've got yourself a deal." She shook his crusty hand. "Now I need a saddle and a horse."

"We can hook you up." A man raised his hand. "I'll bring one around." He left through the parting crowd.

"Thank you. I'll need a scabbard for my musket, too."

"I've got one to lend." Another man turned and ran up the street.

"Bring them to Culpepper's," she hollered, then blushed. Her mother would frown at such an unladylike tone. Grabbing her skirts to keep them out of the mud, she raced through town to the boarding house, her ribs straining against her corset. Her love was in peril. She knew nothing of the terrain and the danger, yet she'd trade her life for Cara and for the man she would marry.

Once in her room, she dressed in her riding habit and her sturdiest boots. Downstairs, she asked Mrs. Culpepper for road-worthy food to take on her ride. She needed medical supplies just in case and…

She almost forgot her gun. Cyrus said to be sure to carry it if the men return. Back upstairs, she found the revolver on the dresser. The grip faced her. She neared the gun. For the first time, she noticed an engraving on the bottom of the pistol grip.

Cyrus said the mark claimed the work. Everything had the mark of the creator.

She picked it up. A large cursive *C* marked swirled in the metal—the same cursive *C* from the letters. A zing shuddered through her. The gun fell from her hands and clattered to the wood floors.

Cyrus! Cyrus wrote those letters? Oh dear, what had she done? But perhaps it was a fluke? She compared the capital *C* to the latest letter. Exact match. The paper trembled in her hand. All their interactions finally clicked into place. All their conversations filled her mind. She knew the connection they shared would be forged in person. Cyrus could never hide his heart from her. Why did he even try?

He knew the thoughts of her heart because he read her letters.

Or maybe he wrote them for Christopher.

How could she be sure Cyrus wrote the letters? Shaking, she slid the gun in her reticule and slung the musket over her shoulder. What if he never came back? She had to ask him. Would she find Cyrus in time?

Chapter 16

Although Maisie rode sidesaddle on her sorrel mare, Molly, with a tiny English saddle many times in the Boston Common, riding cross-country was another matter entirely. Her back ached, and she wasn't used to such a huge Western saddle. But the leaping head propping up her right leg was surprisingly comfortable and made her more confident to push the horse faster.

Rain clouded the horizon and turned the creeks into rivers. Clusters of cottonwoods dotted the banks. Sagebrush whisked the knees of her horse.

"We split right about here." Raking his red hair under his hat, Hanks shifted in his saddle and spit. "Christopher and the other two men went southwest. Cyrus went west, toward Virginia Dale station. Which way are you going?"

Maisie stared at the horizon. Something moved in the distance. Squinting, she focused on the dark spot. She drew out her revolver. Kicking Velvet forward, she rode until the dark spot came into better view.

A man stumbled to the ground.

Cyrus?

"It's Benjamin." Hanks kicked his horse to a canter.

Maisie followed.

"Thank God you came back." Dark red covered Benjamin's leg. His face was milk white, and he trembled all over.

"What happened?" Hanks dismounted, scooped him, and sat on the ground with the wounded man in his arms, propping up his neck.

"Ambushed. We headed to the homestead, and the roughs came up behind us from the north." Shivering, he winced. "They shot me in the leg and Captain Peele in the left arm. I managed to escape. I guess they thought I would die out here anyway." Pointing to a saturated spot on his calf, Benjamin managed a grin. "Quite frankly, I thought I would, too, until I saw you two ride up." He blanched and closed his eyes, rolling his head back onto Hank's chest.

Maisie dismounted, removed the medical supplies from the saddlebags, and knelt in the mud beside Ben. Holding her breath, she tore open his pant leg to expose the wound. She washed away the blood with her drinking water, revealing a circle of burnt flesh. Her stomach turned. She clenched her jaw. To staunch the bleeding, she stuffed the wound with fresh cloth. "Unconscious. He needs medical care." She was torn. Benjamin needed care, but she also wanted to press forward. Maisie stood and placed her hands on her hips. "Honestly, I don't know if I could find my way back. But I'm not sure I can find my way forward."

Hanks gnawed on his plug of tobacco. "Cyrus is still out there. He was following them. If you can catch up, he can bring you back."

"But what about the others?"

Wiping his mouth, Hanks's lips thinned to a straight line. "You can follow that trail to the homestead, or you can find Cyrus. What will you do?"

Nerves needled her stomach. What if she got lost

and was never found? She could easily die out here. She nodded her head west. "I don't know. I don't dare rescue the other men without help."

Hanks grinned with yellowed teeth. "Tell you what, I'll take him back." He bent and lifted Benjamin onto his shoulders.

Benjamin let out a groan.

With furrowed brows, Hank slung him over the saddle. With a rope, he tied him on. "I can't stomach to ride double, and we won't neither ride comfortably. This will be the best option. We'll travel as fast we can."

"Will you send back more men?"

Hanks faced her, his expression pinched. "Lady, I'll be lucky to reach Wylder by nightfall. Riding is one thing. Walking another. By foot, we'll take twice as long. No one will be coming back out tonight. I'd be surprised if you're alive by morning." Hanks spit and sneered. A dark spot blossomed on his shirt where he missed the ground. "You're welcome to return with us, or you can go find your friend."

Maisie bit her lip and studied the terrain.

"Cyrus headed due west. The Overland Trail is well marked, and it will lead you to the station. You can pray he's there. Thanks for the fifty bucks, lady." With that, he led his horse west.

Maisie mounted her horse and gripped the reins. She stared at Hanks's back as he retreated. She could still go with him. It wasn't too late. Facing west, she swallowed hard. The sun poked out of the clouds in intervals. Thunder sounded in the distance. She inhaled and kicked her horse and headed toward Cyrus. In a few yards, she found the trail and followed it until she found the rickety, split-wood cabin. A carved wood sign announced the station. With growing dread in her stomach, she dismounted. Her legs ached. She shook them out and stretched her hips.

A rustle sounded behind her.

Heart thundering, Maisie spun.

Holding two six-shooters, Cyrus bounded out of the trees. He halted, with wide eyes. "Good heavens! What are you doing here? Are you all alone?"

"I—Hanks returned with me—Christopher was ambushed—then we met Benjamin." Words shot out of her. Nerves shook her body. She yearned to run into his arms and hold him.

He furrowed his brows. "Are you hurt?" He rushed forward.

She noticed the blood on her green skirts. "No. Benjamin was shot in the leg. I bandaged him. Hanks took him back home."

"Hanks?" Cyrus frowned.

"He brought me out here and then returned home with the wounded."

Cyrus laughed. "How did you get him to come back out?"

His good eye crinkled almost as much as his scarred eye. "Fifty dollars."

He threw back his head, exposing white teeth.

His laughter sounded louder than anything else in the small copse of trees. She found it rather comforting.

He lowered his head and faced her. "Why did you come?"

"I needed to find my love." She cleared her throat. Would now be a good time to ask him about the mark?

Re-holstering his guns, he shook his head. "You

are either brave or silly."

She thrust out her chin. How dare he insult her pride! "I prefer brave. They were ambushed, you know. Christopher and his two men were heading toward the homestead when Gambell and his men sneaked behind them. The kidnappers headed south. They came from this direction. Christopher was shot."

Cyrus froze. Raising his chin, he lowered his brows. "Is he dead?"

"He was shot in the arm." She tried to see Cyrus as the man who wrote the letters. Was his heart really so tender? Did he care for her, as he often wrote? Or did he write Christopher's dictations? How could she approach such a topic when her friends were in immediate danger?

"We need to plan." Cyrus squatted near a pile of ashes. "When I arrived here, I saw they'd already departed. Food scraps and evidence of a fire and camp were all that remained. They must've eaten a meal here." He stood. "Then they headed southwest."

"You think they're heading for the homestead?"

"If they encountered Christopher, then yes." He bobbed his head. "He was headed there."

His stare warmed her in ways no fire could, yet to admit feelings would draw attention away from the immediate need. "We should ride there and rescue them."

"Hold on there." He caught her arm. "I admire your gumption." He cracked a grin. "But six against two are not odds I favor. And only one of us knows how to shoot properly. Was Hanks sending anyone?"

She shook her head. "He returned on foot. Hanks threw Benjamin over the horse."

Blowing out breath, Cyrus crumpled his brow. "All right. What do you suggest?" He brushed his pants, lifting a gun from its holster. "I say we move out and see where they will stay the night."

Despite her sore hips and bottom, she nodded. "Let's move out. The faster we can get to them, the faster we can get home." But she didn't anticipate returning home to her wedding.

****

When Cyrus spotted Maisie riding through the bushes, he wished her both near and far away. The dual emotions warred inside. Now with her riding beside him, a sense of calm settled over him. A part of his heart wanted to ride away from danger and take her somewhere safe. The other part of him knew she feared for the safety of her friend and fiancé. He could never persuade her to leave them.

The showers continued on and off, and the soft earth made tracking easy, although a few times he dismounted and scouted for signs. When he knelt upon the ground, he laid an ear against the rocky ground,

Maisie lowered her eyebrows. "Are you listening for hoofbeats?"

Cyrus laughed out loud. He raised his head and placed his hands across he knees. "No, I'm looking for anomalies across the ground. Sometimes at ground level, you can see things you can't see from above—a ridge of a print or the shine of an impression."

"Interesting." She tilted her head. "Where did you learn how to track?"

"When I was younger, I learned from my father how to track the animals we hunted." He mounted Salt and Pepper. "Then the US Army trained me to track people."

"You were a scout?"

He dipped his head. Those years are not times he often discussed. The haunting dreams were real enough without having to relive them in words. "That's where I first met Gambell."

"You knew him before the robbery?" Her eyes widened.

Holding his reins in front, he urged Salt and Pepper to a walk. He didn't want to tire his mount. "He didn't want to fight in the war. He complained a good deal and drank even more. A lot of men joined for the paycheck. We were sent ahead to scout enemy troops. One morning, when I was on guard duty, I saw him sneak off. He never returned. Perhaps he's always been a little sore I was the one who reported him to our commanding officer. I don't know if he knew I was the gunsmith in town or if that was a coincidence."

"Oh my!" Maisie opened her lips.

Cyrus placed a hand on his thigh and faced forward. "During the war, we were told to shoot deserters if we saw them again. Shortly after he deserted, I found him in a barn during my furlough. I couldn't go home because I betrayed my father's trust enlisting so young. He still hadn't written me. So I hung close to the army, searching for food." Those were cold and hungry days, paying women for a helping of gruel or whatever they had and scrounging in the pig slop for anything edible. He had money. No one had food.

"What happened when you met him again?"

The undulating rhythm of Salt and Pepper's gait calmed him. "Oh, I didn't kill the man. Maybe I should have. I called him a coward." He checked her reaction.

Maisie widened her eyes. "I bet that went over well."

He huffed. "I was young and foolish. I don't think he ever got over it."

Returning his gaze to the horizon, he led Salt and Pepper up a ridge. A sharp cliff dropped to the right. A swollen river split the low ground in two. A giant barn nestled down below them in a green field beyond. A faint light burned inside. The house was still another few miles away. Perhaps he should ask for help, although he didn't want to drag any more people into this mess. Neither did they have much time. And no lights shone in the house windows.

"We'll have to forge the river." Branches of the creek split in wild ropes of rushing water. Bushes and tree limbs floated in the debris. Cyrus gulped. Crossing a river wasn't his first choice, but it remained their only option. Rainwater gushed down the gully like waterfalls. "Can you descend?" He nodded toward the steep descent.

Maisie nodded and led her horse to the edge.

"You go first." Cyrus led Salt and Pepper behind Maisie. The cliff's shifting red mud tripped his horse. Cyrus leaned far back, holding the reins, moving his weight off the shoulders and onto the horse's croup. Salt and Pepper stumbled underneath him, his front ankles deep in mud.

Maisie's horse fared better.

Salt and Pepper tripped. His front knee landed on a rock. Cyrus held and compensated by holding his body away from the injured foreleg. His horse limped the rest of the way down.

"He's lame." Maisie reined her horse and turned to

face Cyrus. "You can't cross on a lame horse."

Her voice was almost lost against the sound of the flooded beds. Cyrus dismounted and inspected the blood trickling into the mud. He straightened. Coffee-colored water churned nearby. "We can't cross that swollen river without a horse. It's too deep and too powerful."

"We could take turns riding this horse across."

Cyrus chuckled. "I don't know if I could ride side-saddle." Maybe he could take her horse and leave her here with Salt and Pepper, then return when he'd saved the girl and Christopher.

She arched a brow. "You're not leaving me."

Shucks. That woman could read his thoughts. He grinned. "That notion never crossed my mind." A little white lie never hurt anyone. He removed the saddlebags from Salt and Pepper and opened his equine kit. With care, he removed cotton bandages wrapped in oilcloth and pins. He left the small splints and salt water pouch for cleaning eyes in the bag. Wrapping the leg, he stopped the blood flow until he could return to Wylder.

"Could we ride together?"

Staring out to the deluge before him, he gulped. Crossing the river was dangerous for one person. "For a short period of time. We don't want to overtax the horse." No matter how romantic riding double sounded, it wouldn't be comfortable for him or the horse. Closing the kit, he pinned the binding on Salt and Pepper and tied him loosely to a tree branch. Salt and Pepper was good about staying put, but Cyrus also wanted him to get away in case of a wild animal attack. "We won't be long." He stroked its neck and soothed its mane, letting the coarse hair run through his fingers. From his saddlebags, he removed carrots and fed him. The soft hairs of his muzzle tickled his hand. "We should be home before dark." From behind the saddle, he untied his cantle bag in which he kept bundled food and water skins. He swung the leather, dual pannier bags with extra ammo over his shoulder. Then he unsaddled his horse, leaving the saddle on a rock and gave Salt and Pepper a quick brush. Through wavering breaths, he patted the horse one more time. Would it be all right left here on its own? Cyrus had little choice.

He tied his saddlebags onto Maisie's horse. "I'll lead her to the water and then jump on at the last minute."

Maisie nodded, but her gaze held steady on the commotion of the water.

Although at first glance, the river didn't appear to be moving swiftly. Then a whole tree passed in a few seconds. He gulped, his heart racing. Yes. The current was fast. Yes. The current was strong. And if they weren't careful, they'd both wind up downstream or worse.

Chapter 17

Despite the cold weather, Maisie felt her armpits were drenched with sweat. This was probably not the most ladylike thought to cross her mind, and a whole lot more of her would be drenched in a few minutes.

Cyrus led her horse by the bridle into the water.

As energy coursed through her, Maisie held her breath. She wasn't exactly sure this would work. She'd never ridden double before, and crossing a raging river didn't sound like the best time to start.

In a burst of water, Velvet stepped into the current.

Cyrus held her straight.

"Are you climbing on?" She bent to yell over the sound of water.

"Only at the last moment. I don't want to overburden your horse." He led Velvet deeper into the river.

The water darkened the hem of her skirt. Splashes reached the underside of the horse.

Cyrus was near chest-deep in churning water.

Maisie gripped the pommel until her knuckles ached inside her gloves.

Seeing the water reach his armpits, Maisie swallowed hard. Her dampened skirts clung to her knees. "Get on." She couldn't bear to see him ripped away by the chilled water.

But Cyrus pushed through. Debris and branches

brushed his shoulders, and water licked his neck.

He stepped and disappeared below the water. His hat continued downriver.

"Cyrus!" she yelled and searched the water, desperate to see any sign of him. The water bubbled where he dropped. She held her breath, praying for his head to resurface. One breath. Two breaths.

His hatless head poked from the water, dripping. He gasped. His dark hair flattened to his head.

"Climb on!" she shouted.

He grasped the horn and the cantle.

The saddle shifted as he tugged. Maisie snagged an elbow in a futile attempt to help him up.

Neighing, Velvet leg-yielded as the force of the water led her off her straight course.

Clinging to the side of the horse, Cyrus swung his leg over.

His wet arms wrapped around her mid-section. His chest slammed against her back. The touch sent tremors through her for more than one reason. "Are you all right?" she asked over her shoulder.

His face, so near hers, dripped water. "Yes, let's go."

Nearly lip to lip, she passed him the reins. His arms and chest pressed against her sides and back. His cheek was near hers. His chest rose and fell against her ribs. Despite the current danger, a sense of calm rested upon her with him being near. Closeness tugged at her emotions.

The water covered the withers on the horse as she swam neck-deep in the water. When they approached the shore, Velvet climbed the bank, her shoulders moving under their weight.

Once safely on land, Cyrus jumped down. "We'd better light a fire and get dried out."

With his leaving, she felt the full effect of the cold. Near a fallen log, under the canopy of a copse of trees, she dismounted. Moving her joints she returned feeling into her legs and bottom. "I'll search for dry wood." She found a few dry sticks under a fallen branch and brought them back.

Cyrus gathered kindling and, with a flint and knife, knelt and worked the stone until it produced a spark. At last, he coaxed a small fire into existence. "We can't stay long. We don't know when they'll leave, but we need a plan."

This was the first time she'd sat on his right side. The full effects of his scar were in full view. His face didn't seem as repulsive as when she first met him. Indeed, she hardly noticed the scars at all. In fact, his heart outshone any imperfection in his face. His brooding stare turned her heart. She could never just ask him about the letters. No, indeed. For she was sure he would never admit to it. She'd have to be cleverer than that. He knew her. He knew her like no one else ever had. He resonated on the same string. Two notes of their souls played in harmony. His heart echoed her own feelings. How could she provoke him to confess those admissions? She couldn't force him to admit to the lie. She'd have to be sly about it. Maisie cleared her throat. "I do miss my mother. She was the sweetest thing." Even to herself, her voice sounded pinched. She sneaked a glance at Cyrus.

"I'm sorry to hear that." But his expression didn't change. Nor did he give any indication he'd read her letters complaining of her mother's oppressiveness.

Drat! She'd have to try a different tack.

****

If Cyrus hadn't known any better, he would've guessed that Miss Maisie lost her mind in the cold. Praising her mother for her sweetness and tenderness went against everything she wrote in her letters. Sitting on a damp log near the fire, he pinched his lips to keep from correcting her or commenting on the inaccuracies of her statements. She revealed those secrets in letters to Christopher, not himself. He'd been so careful not to talk about anything that stirred in his heart or how deeply her words embedded inside him.

Dusk brushed against the horizon on the west. Clouds blurred the moon and gave an unearthly glow to the sagebrush. Their clothes dried. With gun in hand, Cyrus crept up to a small ridge separating them from the barn. The large bank barn was like many others in the area and wide enough inside to turn around a wagon. It was cut into the hill, with a stone mason footing. Rough-planed planks filled in the rest. A tall, sloping, gambrel-style hip roof crowned its head. Ventilation windows for the hay loft faced him. Nine horses pawed near the posts outside. Cyrus bent. "How do you think we ought to rescue them?"

Maisie furrowed her brow. "Is there a back door?"

"Usually barns this size have two entrances. One at the front and one at the back for animals. I'll tell you what. I'll check and see what is going on inside. Stay here."

"I'm going with you."

Cyrus nodded. He needed her near. And he couldn't keep her back now. "Stay low." He crossed the landscape.

Maisie gasped.

Cyrus glanced back. Her skirt had caught in a bush. He ripped it free. After a few paces, he realized he grabbed her hand. Thrilling sensations patted through him. At a vertical ventilation slit, he ducked so his shadow wouldn't be seen. Slowly, he peered through a ventilation slat cut in the side of the large bank barn.

Shouts floated out on the breath of the wind's sigh.

Near the back of the barn, unsaddled horses neighed in the stalls. Straw or hay littered the floor. In the shadows, Cyrus made out a plow collar on a large wooden peg hanging over the overturned spidery legs of a rusty harrow, tin buckets, no doubt filled with feed, and a stool.

Back near a horse stall, Christopher sagged against a wood pillar, tied round his chest with a rope. The wound from his left arm blossomed blood all over the sleeve of his blue uniform.

To the left, the other volunteer lay.

On Christopher's right, Cara sat, bound with her hands on her lap. Her jaw trembled, and her eyes were as wide as barrels.

One of the captors, Slouchy, leaned against his saddle on the floor with saddle blankets underneath them—catching a wink of shut-eye. His hat covered his face, his legs crossed at the ankles, and his hands folded across the chest.

Stinky leaned against a large sack of grain, his back toward the front door. Three more men stood near the red lantern.

"We should just kill them all off now." Talks-Too-Loud paced. The floorboards creaked under his boots. "We can't take all three of them to Silver City."

Red Beard gestured toward Christopher. "Are you kidding me? This one has a uniform of a Calvary officer. I don't want no trouble with no Calvary. I don't want them coming after us."

"We can't have three extra mouths to feed. Keeping prisoners is too risky." Talks-Too-Loud gestured with outstretched arms.

Their shadows danced around the wooden walls filled with farming bric-a-brac.

"Three extra riders would slow us down." Slouchy opened his eyes.

"What do you suggest?" Red Beard faced Slouchy and walloped him. "We can't leave them. They've overheard our plans. We can kill this one, at least." He gestured toward the volunteer. "He ain't no officer."

Talks-Too-Loud pointed toward Cara. "And the woman we have to take with us…"

"Wait until Gambell returns." Red Beard stomped a foot.

Outside, Cyrus sank into the dirt, leaning against the exterior wall. He'd heard enough. "They're fighting amongst themselves. Seems like taking Christopher captive was an act of defensive behavior rather than a planned offensive. But sadly, they do want Cara. And if we don't act now, they'll kill the other volunteer."

"What can we do?"

The desperation in her voice compelled him to come up with something. He brushed a thumb against his lip. "They've got the prisoners in the back. The men are sleeping up front."

"I'll sneak around the back and release Christopher and Cara. What do you think?"

Urgency laced her whispers. Her whole face

crumpled. Cyrus admired how much she cared for her friend and fiancé. He nodded. "I'll go in the front as a distraction."

"Can you take on six men?"

He released his gun from his holster and shrugged. "I have before."

"But this time they have your guns. And we're not in town. We're out in the middle of nowhere."

He bit his lip. True, but he had the advantage of surprise.

"If you need help fending off the men, I'll tell Christopher to return with my gun and help you."

The idea of Christopher helping him sounded as fun as dying. "No, he's been hurt. Once you untie him, get them out, saddle their horses, and lead them back home."

"I'm not sure I could get them home."

"Even semi-conscious, Christopher will know the way."

She nodded with large, dark blue eyes. How he admired her gumption. She would march into a den of thieves and snatch her lover from the jaws of Hell. Too bad the lover was Christopher.

"And what will you do? You could die in there."

Without Maisie, his life would be as lifeless as death. "Don't worry about me. Ride as fast as you can and get your friends safe." He wasn't planning to live through this fight.

"What about you?"

Her concern tore at him. His heart yearned for her all the more. "I'll be fine." He hoped he sounded more confident than he felt. If only he could kiss her goodbye.

"Here, take my handgun as an added measure." She grabbed her revolver and handed it over.

He dug his jackknife out of his pocket and folded her hand around it. Her hands were sure and capable. He wished he could hold onto her for forever. "You'll need a blade to cut those cords. Be careful." He squeezed her hand again for the last time.

With the knife, she headed downhill toward the southern side of the barn. Then she disappeared around the corner.

Leaning his head against the barn, Cyrus inhaled deeply. Would this be his last act alive?

Chapter 18

Without so much as a breath of noise, Maisie crept inside the barn. Goats, chickens, and a few pigs crawled in the dirt alongside her below the main floor of the barn. The heady scent of animal feed and droppings hit her with full force. Raising an eyebrow, she covered her nose with a hand as she ducked into the darkened space cut out of the stone masonry. She picked up her skirts as much as possible. The temperature warmed as she was now out of the wind, but the stench of animal increased as she tramped through mud—at least she hoped it was mud—up to her ankles where the animals trod. She preferred facing kidnappers head on with the threat of a gunfire rather than stepping in animal waste.

Wooden stairs led up toward the dim light coming from a square cut in the plank floors. All those years sneaking out of the house taught her to walk on the tread closest to the supports as it was the quietest place to step without making a noise. She placed her muddy boots on the outer edges of the steps and hiked up her soiled skirts.

Gulping back fear, she reached the main floor of the barn. Now she had to find Christopher and Cara and the other volunteer gentleman. She stepped into the feed room, partitioned from the rest of the barn by an eight-foot wall of wooden planks. Hooks with tack and bridles hung from the posts holding it up. Her eyes grew accustomed to the dark. To the left, horses snorted. A few barrels filled most of the room which was about six feet wide and ran the width of the back part of the barn. The partition stopped about four feet from the other wall, leaving an opening. Pulling on her skirts, she knelt on all fours and peered around the corner.

About nine feet away, Cara sat near another barrel of feed, bound hand and foot. Her usually well-kept red locks hung in a scraggly mess. A bruise purpled her right cheekbone. Maisie could only see Christopher's back, but his uniform was dark on his left shoulder. He leaned his head against a wooden beam supporting the roof. Ropes encircled his chest, holding him against the beam. Only the boots of the other man resting on the straw-strewn floor were visible.

Gambell's men argued about twenty feet away in the front of the barn. A red, hot-blast lantern on the floor offered a little light.

Cara's profile was half-facing her. Perhaps she could get her attention. Behind the partition, Maisie waved her arms. Cara's eyes remained large, but her gaze never wavered from Christopher.

Maisie found a lump of something which she hoped was mere mud and rolled it toward Cara.

The lump caught her eye. She lifted her head. Her eyebrows rose. Her nose turned pink, and her eyes reddened. Her lips parted.

Maisie raised a finger to her mouth to shush her. Though Gambell's men continued to argue and seemed to be occupied, she didn't want to draw their attention.

A smile spread across Cara's cracked lips.

Maisie motioned to come a little closer so she

could untie her in the darkened corner of the stall rather than right there in the light.

Slowly, Cara scooted closer toward the post where Christopher was tied near the stall. Then she stretched her feet near Maisie.

In the shadows of the wall, Maisie used Cyrus's knife to cut the ropes off Cara's legs. Red rope burn circled her ankles. Maisie tried to be gentle.

Cara's eyebrows folded. She hitched her breath.

Maisie bit her lip. At last, Cara's feet were free.

She scooted closer.

Maisie worked on her wrists.

Cara was free.

Maisie pointed toward the animal entrance behind and below them.

Cara nodded and slid across the wooden floor until she reached the stairs.

Now for Christopher. Leaning close to his broad shoulders, she noticed the blood soaking the hay on the floor. She touched him gently.

He jerked his head.

His lips were parched and cracked. A pallor blanched his face. He opened his mouth.

Maisie shook her head and placed a finger to her lips. She worked on his hands and the ropes around his chest. Carrying an injured man by herself would be impossible. She leaned close to his ear. "You're free." She lowered her voice to the faintest of whispers. "Don't say anything. Just blink if yes and lower your brows for no. Can you walk?"

He lowered his brows. Then he blinked.

She should've picked different signals. How could she tell if he was thinking with the furrowed brows or if he changed his mind? "Is your friend still alive?" She couldn't see anything of him except a pair of boots sticking out from his legs. Christopher blocked the rest of him.

A blink.

Relief filtered through her. "Is he fit to travel?"

A blink again.

Some good news. She risked a wavering breath. Without a distraction, she couldn't get Christopher out or untie their friend.

As if on cue, the door slammed on the other side of the barn.

Maisie risked a glance toward the front door.

Cyrus stood there with two guns drawn, ready for a fight.

Despite the shadows casting grotesque shapes across his scarred face, he never looked more glorious or handsome at that time. Warmth spread through her. She never loved him more.

****

Cyrus relished the element of surprise. "Good evening, boys." He wished he had a hat to tip. His hands held guns anyway.

The two on the floor jumped to their feet, and the three standing around the red, hot-blast lantern immediately reached for their guns.

The foremost stepped forward. "What do you want?"

Oh, yeah. His name was Talks-Too-Loud.

Cyrus pocketed his guns and raised his hands to the sky. "No need to get antsy. I just came to retrieve that which is my own." He was vulnerable holstering his guns, but the act would intrigue them and keep low the tension. The dark-haired man's bloodshot gaze followed him like a hawk's. Cyrus fought to keep his attention off Maisie sawing through the ropes of the volunteer in the shadows.

A hint of kerosene smoke and whiskey tinged Cyrus's nose. An open bottle sat on a barrel. "You boys been having a good time?" Cyrus stalled.

Maisie and the volunteer hauled Christopher back into the darkness. He only needed a few more minutes before he'd have to start firing. A whiff of body odor wafted past his nose.

"Don't we know you?" Stinky lifted his chin.

Red Beard stumbled forward. "Yeah. You're the gunsmith." He raised his gun. "With the ugly face." Grinning with broken teeth, the man taunted with a gun.

Cyrus's fingers itched. He could draw quicker and outshoot all of them, especially with their senses dulled with liquor, but he wanted to wait until Maisie and the others were safely away before the gunfight started. A stray bullet could easily penetrate these thin boards or exit through a ventilation slit. And if he didn't make it out alive, he wanted to make sure she had time enough to escape. "Remember our last encounter when you six called me ugly." For the first time, Cyrus counted the men. Only five men in the barn. Where was Gambell? "Now, I've come to even the score. One on one."

"You're not so tough without your hammer, are you?" Slouchy called.

But Red Beard made the first move. Swinging in with clumsy haymakers, Red Beard made his way toward Cyrus.

Cyrus dropped him with an uppercut to his chest.

Thundering across the planks, Talks-Too-Loud

charged with his head lowered.

Side-stepping his angry bull motions easily, Cyrus clasped his hands together and pummeled Talks-Too-Loud with a double fist to the back.

He flattened to the floor.

Cyrus picked him up by neck and crop and rammed him, head first, into the wall.

Talks-Too-Loud fell silent and unconscious near a feed bag.

Wiping his brow, Cyrus readied for the next attack. Panting, he inched away from a plow share in the corner and clenched his throbbing fists. Cyrus rolled his neck. "Who's next?"

Greasy staggered closer with a drunken stupor. His bloodshot eyes rolled in his sockets.

Then Slouchy and Stinky joined the fray.

Cyrus spun around the three men. He wasn't sure how long Maisie and the others would take to get away, but he hoped he could keep up this fight.

****

With thundering heart, Maisie caught up to the others hiding between the horses. "I'm returning to help Cyrus." She rolled the hem of her cuirass and imagined all sorts of bad things that could happen to him alone in there with all those men. Although she was sure he could hold his own, he might need back up.

"Want me to stay behind as well?" The friend settled Christopher on the ground near the hitching post while he saddled the horses.

Christopher breathed heavy, the rise and fall of his shoulders slow.

"No. You need to make sure Christopher and Cara make it back safely." She knelt beside Christopher.

Taking up the dust ruffle of her dress, she cut off a clean part of her underskirts. She leaned into Christopher. The scent of damp wool rose to her nose. With great gentleness, she wrapped the cloth around his arm. "To staunch the bleeding."

Christopher's eyes shone in the dim light. "You're staying with him, aren't you?"

Nodding, Maisie focused on tying the knot around his left arm—hard enough to stop the flow of blood but not enough to cause him pain.

"You know, he wrote the letters."

His words barely came out in a whisper. "I know." She faced him, finished with the temporary bandage. "Why didn't you write them yourself?"

"I didn't have the words." He rocked his head slightly. "I was afraid you wouldn't want me and wouldn't come." His gaze flicked past her. "Everything worked out better than I expected."

Maisie followed his line of sight.

Cara held the reins, ready to go. She returned his shy grin.

"She likes you, you know. She has for a while."

He bowed his head, then raised it. "What about you? You love him, don't you? You said you loved the man who wrote the words."

She touched a brass button. "Yes, I do."

"I knew you didn't love me. At first it hurt. I was jealous of Cyrus. But now I see things in a different light. You are meant for each other."

With the help of Cara and the friend, she saddled Christopher's horse. "We left Cyrus's horse tied up on the other side of the river. It's flooded. We'll meet you there. If we're not there by morning, ride back to

Wylder for help."

Nodding, the friend helped Christopher up into the saddle. The friend took the reins and mounted his own horse and hightailed it up the ridge toward the river.

Maisie helped Cara mount the horse.

"Thank ye ever so much!" Cara's cheekbone was still bruised, but her eyes were no longer dim.

"No time to talk. Be off."

Cara stayed behind. "Aren't ye comin', Maisie?"

"I'll be along shortly." Maisie walked alongside Cara's horse to the copse of trees where her own horse waited patiently. Her saddle was over the log. She found her flintlock, the powder horn, and ammo bag. With her hands full, she tucked the knife into her corset for safe-keeping.

Cara bobbed her head. "Yer not comin' with us, are ye?"

Maisie glanced over her shoulder in the direction of the barn. "I'm going back for Cyrus. He hasn't returned."

"Cyrus?" Her eyes flattened to slits with her smile.

"He's here too. He led the rescue."

"I see." Cara shifted in her saddle. She led the horse toward the others. "Be safe."

"I'll try." But when did she ever listen to people when they gave her advice? Turning her back to Cara, she placed the powder horn over her shoulder.

Power from her muzzleloader emboldened her. She straightened her spine. Yet an icy trickle of fear rushed in her stomach. She stepped into the stockyard toward the glowing barn. Light shone from the vertical ventilation slits along the sides.

A figure emerged across the stockyard.

Maisie ducked into the shadows and kept her gaze on the figure.

Closer to the barn, his face grew recognizable.

Gambell. Maisie sucked in her breath. Why wasn't he already in the barn?

****

Across the barn floor, Stinky raged forward.

Cyrus jabbed him in the left side of his neck.

Stinky fell backward. The drink probably dropped him more than the punch.

"You think you're so tough, gunsmith?" Greasy grabbed Cyrus around the shoulders, pinning down his arms.

Slouchy got in a sucker punch.

"Ouf." Cyrus would've doubled over from the blossoming pain in his gut, but Greasy held him fast from behind.

Slouchy stepped closer for a second hit.

After head-butting Slouchy, Cyrus dropped all his weight to the ground and rolled back onto Greasy and elbowed him in the ribs.

Greasy released his grip. "Ugh." He clutched his stomach.

Cyrus elbowed him in the jaw and stood then kicked him in the chest with the heel of his boot.

Greasy rolled to his side.

Slouchy tackled Cyrus into the plow share in the corner.

Pain tore across his right flank. *That's gonna leave a bruise.*

Slouchy pinned him there, grappling Cyrus's hands behind his back.

Utilizing all his strength, Cyrus pushed himself off

the plowshare with his legs and spun his weight to control Slouchy. Cyrus landed him against the wall and sandwiched Slouchy between the wall and his body. Cyrus head-butted him again.

Slouchy released him.

Cyrus spun and hit him in the chest. He surveyed the room. Nobody moved.

Only Greasy rolled on the floor, clutching his mid-section.

Cyrus watched him, ready to take him on again when he felt something cold against the back of his neck.

"Well, if it isn't my old friend, the gunsmith."

Gambell's teeth clicked when he talked. Cyrus's throat tightened. He watched Gambell from the corner of his eye. The revolting smell of onions and body odor tumbled out with whiskey fumes on his breath. Cyrus worried about lighting a match.

"Your guns have made us mighty rich men. I thank you." After a slight bow, Gambell cast his bloodshot eyes around the barn. He pressed the gun into his neck.

Only Greasy stirred. Glaring, he stood and clutched his chest.

Slouchy rolled over and slowly got to his feet.

Gambell spat onto the floor. "I see you've taught my boys a lesson. You've given me quite a problem to solve here, figuring out how to transport four unconscious men. At least you've saved me the trouble of disposing of three prisoners." His crooked grin flashed in the lantern light.

His mouth was configured with mismatched teeth. Still, he looked better than the toothless version of his mouth the last time they met. Maybe. No, never mind.

The addition of the oversized teeth did nothing for his appearance.

"You saved us the trouble of killing them. You will not be so lucky."

Good—they got away. Maisie was safe. Relief washed over him. Now he would die in peace.

"We'll be long gone before they make it to civilization. No one's at the homestead. Now I gotta figure out what to do with you." His chuckle came from deep within his throat. "I just wish I'd had my revenge on that sweet, little black-haired tart."

Cyrus clenched his jaw. Instinctively, he jerked his hands, ready to mangle this man.

Gambell pressed the barrel into his neck harder. "Tie him up."

Cyrus dropped his hands. At least Maisie was miles away. And safe.

****

Maisie was less than twenty feet from Cyrus. She sneaked in the animal entrance and crept up the stairs. Taking stock of her assets, she had Cyrus's knife, held in her bodice for safe-keeping, and her great-great-great-grandfather's musket that wasn't even gifted by the great Lafayette. Her prospects didn't seem so great. Crouching, she leaned her musket against the stall wall and peeked around the corner.

Just to the side of the lantern, Gambell held Cyrus at gunpoint. The lantern threw nasty shadows all over the beams, the stalls, and the farming equipment. But the nastiest was Gambell's himself. A sneer cut across his face like a slit. "Tie him up."

The dark, greasy-haired man hunched on a barrel clutching his stomach. Grabbing a length of rope, he dismounted his seat and forced Cyrus down.

Gambell flattened his eyes to slits. "Remember no funny business. I have my gun on you."

Her throat tightened. Seeing Cyrus in the hands of those awful men soured her stomach. Maisie needed a plan. She leaned back out of sight, accidentally bumping the musket. Reaching out her hand, she tried to grab it before it fell to the floor. It clattered into a bucket in a noisy ruckus.

Oh, why did she bring the darn thing? Her heartbeat thundered in her ears.

"Go check it out," Gambell said.

Energy spiked through her. She didn't have time to load the flintlock. A man could easily overpower any attempt at attack. Where could she hide? A darkened corner of the barn held an oiled cloth. She ducked under the cloth and tucked her feet under her. Her dark riding habit was some level of camouflage.

The floorboards groaned as someone drew closer. Footsteps scraped along the straw on the floor.

Her heartbeat sounded so loud, she swore it could be heard. She dared not breathe. Cozy heat surrounded her.

Then the cloth flew off.

Cold wind whooshed up with it. Her sweat turned to ice. Before her stood the greasy, dark-haired man.

"Gotcha." He dug his grip into her arms and yanked her upright.

Caught! Terror spiked her heartbeat. Maisie found her feet. She'd left her gun on the floor.

He half-dragged, half-carried her out of the stall and into the light of the kerosene lantern sitting in the middle of the spacious barn.

Why did she think she could help Cyrus? All she did was make the situation worse. Maisie gulped. Icy fear raked through her. Before she was within a few feet of him, she smelled Gambell—reeking of onions, garlic, and sweat mixed with whiskey. His odd-sized teeth hung like tombstones from his mouth. Hideous shadows played across his face as he grimaced.

Gambell raised his gun to her neck. "Look what I found. I carry away a maid and get the princess in exchange. It's my lucky night." He licked his lips.

Bile rose to Maisie's throat.

The greasy man held her arms tight behind her. A slouching man in the corner trained his gun on Cyrus.

"No!" Cyrus yelled.

In one quick move, Gambell yanked her closer. "She's mine now."

He snaked her hand behind her back. His breath bore down upon her neck, and the stench of his body odor and alcohol nearly made her pass out. Powerlessness and dread grew in her heart.

"If you touch her…" Cyrus strained against his bands. His back was against a pillar.

"You'll what?" Gambell parted his dry lips, exposing his mismatched teeth in a bark of laughter.

Cyrus's gaze burned. "You'll pay. I promise you'll regret being born."

The slouchy man knocked his head then trained his gun on Maisie.

"I will enjoy this." Gripping the top of her collar, Gambell ripped open her riding habit jacket and white undershirt.

Buttons fell to the floor and rolled across the planks.

Cool air brushed against her exposed skin. Angry tears pricked her eyes. She stamped on his boots and kicked her captor's shins. She elbowed the greasy man behind her. But he still held her arms.

Gambell shook his finger. "Ah, ah! No kicking."

His teeth made a weird clicking sound when he spoke.

"Or I will be the last person you see."

Tremors shot through her. What a repulsive thought! Her heart rate doubled.

He sneered. "See you can be a tame mare."

She closed her eyes. Her mother always said her impulsiveness would kill her. This just might be the day.

****

Cyrus felt as though he'd swallowed a cannon ball. Gambell's pale green eyes shone with wicked delight. If his grimy hands so much as touch Maisie, he would suffer a miserable death. Anger fueled a fire in Cyrus's chest. "Let her go! This feud is between you and me."

"I don't think so. This girl shot me in the arm. It will never be the same. I want just compensation."

For the first time, Cyrus noticed Gambell's lame arm never moved.

Maisie leaned forward and bit Gambell's lame arm. "You'll get no pleasure out of me!"

"You she-goat!" He roared and lowered the gun to her head.

"Noooo!" Cyrus gasped for breath. He had no wish to see Maisie murdered. Heat rose in his chest. "Don't you dare!"

With venom in his eyes, Gambell hugged his arm. "Tie her up with the other one."

Greasy dragged her to the post and tied her hands behind her next to Cyrus.

Narrowing his eyes, Cyrus puffed his chest. "Why are you doing this?"

Gambell curled his lip, exposing rotten teeth. "I want to see you both suffer in the most horrible way possible."

Cyrus's heart sickened. Why didn't Maisie go with the others? She kicked and squirmed, but both Greasy and Slouchy held her firm and tied their knots sure.

Maisie's eyes grew large. "And how will you do that?"

Gambell threw back his head and cackled. "I won't shoot you, I'll tell you that. Gunshots are over too quickly—too painless."

Cyrus leaned closer. "Are you okay?" he whispered.

Maisie nodded.

Her hair had come out of her up-do and curled around her neck. Her eyebrows peaked in the center of her forehead. He yearned to comfort her. "You were very brave."

Gambell took a swig from the whiskey bottle. "You don't know how much these teeth hurt. I have sores all over the inside of my mouth. Every time I eat, it tears at my gums. The only thing that dulls the pain is liquor." He took a drink and grinned over the top of his bottle. "And seeing you suffer."

Greasy gathered the saddles and horse blankets. Then, with help from Slouchy, he hauled the fallen men outside.

Cyrus kept his focus on Gambell. "Did the others get away?" he whispered to Maisie.

She nodded.

"Why didn't you?"

Her gaze rose to his. "I couldn't leave you."

A zing of pleasure unlike anything he'd ever experienced pierced him. Her expression of earnestness stirred respect and admiration.

She bit her lip. "But all I have done is put us in a more precarious situation."

"Nonsense." Strength battled through. Being loved gave him a will to overcome all odds. If she asked him, he would destroy all these men to save her. Before she walked into the barn, he expected to die for her. Now he had every intention of living. "We will get out of this."

"You have a personal credo, do you not? 'Victory favors the virtuous.' "

"How did you know?" Heat rose to his collar. Realization dawned. The letters. She knew. He closed his eyes. "When did you realize?" He lowered his voice.

"Only just before I left Wylder. I noticed the mark on your guns and the closing of your letters were the same. But honestly, that was just confirmation. I knew in my heart Christopher could not write such letters. Your words connected with my heart. You couldn't hide such a connection. One cannot hide a heart."

Despite the ruffians' general looting of the barn and the horses, Cyrus was riveted to her words. He leaned his head against the post.

She settled her head on his shoulder. "I told Christopher I was in love with the man who wrote the letters."

That would explain why Christopher was so angry.

Jealousy overruled his good sense. At least the ruffians left the lamp so Cyrus could see to bust them out with no problem.

Gambell opened the door once more. "I have one more goodbye present." He grabbed a branding iron from the corner and stuck it in the kerosene lamp flame.

Cyrus kept his gaze on that iron. If they even touch Maisie…

When it glowed orange, Gambell removed the iron. He crossed the floor with the bottle of whiskey in his lame arm and the blazing orange iron in the other. "Now the left side of your face will be as ugly as the right."

Cyrus backed against the post, heart thundering in his chest. Gambell was crazy or drunk. Or both.

Gambell was about three steps from Cyrus.

Maisie thrust out a leg.

Gambell tumbled. The iron dropped from his hand, igniting a bit of straw on fire and leaving a scorch mark on the wood floor.

Three small, white things tumbled to the planking.

His teeth. Cyrus bit back a laugh.

Grabbing up his teeth, Gambell cursed and stumbled to get himself upright with his good arm. The smell of whiskey overpowered any other smell. Once on his feet, he faced Cyrus. "Damn you." Then, backing away from the two of them, he lowered his gun. "This will have to do." And he shot the kerosene lamp.

The lantern burst into flames. The straw on the floor immediately lit. Fire spread around the barn. Fear prickled Cyrus's neck. He shot a glance toward Maisie. How could he save her?

****

Flame crackled across the room. As horror crawled up her spine, Maisie tucked her feet under her skirts.

Oil from the lantern pooled on the floor and caught fire.

Gambell opened the barn doors, letting in a whoosh of cool air, flaming the sparks. He tapped his gun to the brim of his hat. "Ay-di-ous!" The door shut behind him.

"What shall we do?" Maisie held her breath against her tremors. The flame crawled across the floor toward her, igniting the straw. Soon, the sparks would catch the wood on fire, and then they'd have a real problem.

"See if you can untie your ropes." Cyrus worked his wrists.

She twisted the ropes until her wrists burned. If only... *The knife.* "Cyrus, I have your knife. Tucked into my bodice. Do you think you could reach it?"

Cyrus raised his eyebrows. He cast her a sideways gaze. "Where exactly?"

She lowered her gaze to the center of her chest. "In the safest place I could put it." Then she faced him. "Do you think you could..." She gulped. "Do you think you could, if I turned toward you, perhaps snatch it from my corset?"

He lowered his eyebrows. "How would I do that?"

Her face burned. "Well, it's wedged between...You'd have to use, um, maybe use your teeth."

Setting his head back against the post, he faced forward. Color tinted his cheeks. "I'd rather die."

Smoke curled around her. Maisie coughed. Across from them, a feed sack caught fire. She stamped the heel of her boot into the floor. "This is no time for prudish virtue. We will burn!" Using her feet she twisted around and raised her chest to Cyrus.

He raised his shoulders then nodded. Twisting as far as he could with his hands tied behind him, he lowered his face into her bosom.

"I don't see it."

His breath warmed her skin. She held her breath. "I promise. It's down there."

He breathed again, tickling her chest.

At last, he lowered his face into the fluffy folds of her underclothing.

Warmth from his face brushed against her. He rummaged around with his chin. His unshaven cheeks brushed delicate skin. The feeling was not unpleasant.

At last, he emerged with the knife between his teeth.

Sheepishness filled his face. She didn't have time for his embarrassments. "Hurry."

Flames licked the walls. Smoke rose to the ceiling.

He tossed his head.

The knife fell into her hands behind her. Either heat from the room or from the embarrassment reddened his face. Not being able to see made using the knife tricky. Sweat pricked her body. She held the knife awkwardly in her hands, pressing it against the ropes and worked the blade back and forth across the bindings. Her hand cramped.

"Is it working?"

"I've got it." As the smoke accumulated around her, she coughed. The knife grew sweaty in her hands and slipped from her fingers. "Oh, no!" Clenching her jaw, she tugged on the ropes. They strained against her wrists. Leaning into the post for leverage, she pulled until her shoulders ached.

The flames licked the floor near her and blazed across the room. Dark clouds of smoke curled above them. Horses whinnied and neighed.

The ropes popped. She snatched the knife. Holding her cuff to her nose to block the smoke, she turned to saw through Cyrus's ropes. Once he was free, she handed him the knife.

With one slice, he cut through the ropes at her ankles and then his own. He stood and held out his hand.

She grasped it and stood, then she ducked again on the floor. "Get down." Crawling across the scorched floor, she reached the door. It wouldn't budge. She yelled and batted the door with her fists.

"Blocked from the outside."

She examined the inferno behind her. Through the smoke, she noticed the darkness of the animal entrance. "We can get out the back."

"Wrap your shirt over your nose." He removed his shirt and covered his face. "And run."

Without hesitation, she lifted her mass of skirts over her nose. What would her mother say if she saw her now? Maisie was lost in a blaze of heat and smoke. At last she came to the cooler side of the barn. She opened the stalls for the horses to escape. The wind blew up gusts from the animal entrance below.

"My musket!" She snatched the bag, the powder horn, and the gun.

Cyrus pulled out her six-shooter from his boot.

She followed him out the back way into the cool depths of the barn. "We can't let them get away." Her cheeks smarted from the fire. Parts of her dress burned. Outside, the cold bit into her. She clutched together the edges of her bodice. Holding his hand, she raced up the hill toward the horses. She peeked around the corner.

Gambell and two of his men stood by their horses, tying unconscious men onto saddles.

"We can take them." She squinted into the darkness.

Wind blew his dark hair around his forehead. "We have two guns, and they have three men."

"We can't let them escape." Justice must be served. Setting her jaw, she held out her hands. "They have to stand trial. They kidnapped Cara and Christopher. Gambell wanted them killed. And he tried to kill us."

He caught her hand. "If we confront them, this won't end in a trial. It will end in a gunfight. Are you prepared for those consequences? I am willing to accompany you to the ends of the earth. If necessary, I would lay down my life for you."

His gaze bored into hers.

Maisie inhaled smoke and fresh air. "Didn't you once write, 'Heroes never seek nor shun a fight' in one of your letters?"

A smile graced his lips. "Using my words against me."

She gripped his hand and stared into his eyes. "We have to stop them for Cara and Christopher."

He leaned against the barn and nodded. "Load your flintlock like how I showed you. Have it ready to go. Once the shots start, you won't have time to find your ammunition."

Maisie trapped the gun between her knees and hauled out the wadding and lead balls from her bag.

He stood near the stone corner of the burning barn and kept an eye on the criminals as they hefted bags on the horses. "Remind me to get you ready-made cartridges for the muzzleloader."

Clutching the gun, she pulled back the new hammer, lifted up the frizzen, and poured a few grains of black powder into the flash pan. Then she set the frizzen. She loaded the ball and the wadding into the muzzle and tamped it down with the pin. While she was no revolutionary, living out West certainly changed her. She was no longer afraid.

"Once that's cocked, it's ready to go. Don't fire until you have to. You only have one shot."

Hitching up the gun to her shoulder well, Maisie nodded. She stepped past the burning barn and into the stockyard. She wanted her dress back and for them to pay for what they did to her friends.

Chapter 19

Cyrus's mouth was as dry as a black powder. Confronting Gambell himself didn't scare him. Having Maisie with him complicated matters and added additional risk. He would've preferred to leave Maisie behind, but she would've insisted on coming. And he couldn't stop her. Despite the cold, he smiled, sweat prickling his body. She was so adorable in her singed dress. Determination flashed in her eyes. And that musket. As they crossed the field behind a cow, she clung to it.

A cow was not his most ideal cover, but it was all they had.

Light from the fire behind him lit up the criminals. Cyrus aimed at Slouchy's legs. The sound of gunshot echoed off the barn behind him and sounded into the night.

Slouchy fell to the dust with a thud.

The cow ran, clanging its bell, bellowing a loud *moooooo*.

Gambell ducked behind his horse. Only he and Greasy remained.

A shot hit the dirt beside Cyrus. "This way." He grabbed Maisie by the arm and ducked behind the wooden water trough, about two feet high and six feet long.

Another shot hit the side. Water gushed out,

soaking the ground beneath him.

Rising up on his knees, he cleared a shot over the water, but it was a wild shot. He didn't have time to see where Gambell or Greasy hid. "Gambell, come out. You can't hide forever." Heat from the fire burned at his back.

"I can stay here all night if I have to."

"But your buddies can't. They need medical care, and you know it. The minute you try to get on your horse, I'll shoot you. So come out with your hands up. Turn yourself into the law."

At the sounds of hoofbeats, Cyrus peered over the top of the water trough. Gambell released the horses with his unconscious friends.

Only Gambell and Greasy remained.

Cyrus peeked again. Gambell hid behind his horse. Beyond them was a grove of trees. Cyrus didn't see Greasy.

"You can't make it out of here alive," Gambell shouted. "We are taking all the horses. You can try at the homestead, but I guarantee you, they won't answer." Laughing, Gambell taunted them across the stockyard. "You'll die either way."

"Go ahead and try to leave. Once you get on your horse, I'll pick you off, like cans on a log."

Gambell grabbed the saddle horn.

Aiming from his crouch, Cyrus shot him. The sound echoed in the dark.

Gambell fell to the ground, crumpling a small sagebrush.

Horses whinnied and pulled on their tethers.

Three shots down. Three shots left. Cyrus stood.

With his gun across the saddle, Greasy shot from

behind a horse.

Cyrus ducking and pivoting to see clearly, shot him.

With a cry, Greasy fell against the wooden pole with a *thunk* and slid to the ground.

Kneeling, Cyrus nodded to Maisie. "Stay here. I'll check it out and make sure they're dead." Tentatively, he stalked around the water trough. The ground turned to mud near the bullet hole. He kept his gaze on the men on the ground.

Gambell's face contorted in the dancing flames.

Cyrus couldn't tell if he breathed or not. Keeping his gun at the ready, he waited for any movement.

Greasy lay facedown.

Where was he shot?

In a blink, Greasy rose to his elbow, a sneer on his face. His gun wasn't pointed at Cyrus but at an angle behind him.

In horror, Cyrus realized where he pointed his gun. He jumped in front of Maisie while aiming his gun for Greasy's chest, then pulled the trigger. Two gunshots rang in the air—one right after another.

Greasy fell.

While in mid-air, a ball hit Cyrus. A burn zinged through his upper right arm. He fell to the earth.

****

Maisie didn't remember screaming. When Cyrus fell to the ground, her voice echoed off the barn. Was he dead?

Another shot rang out. She stood.

Gambell struggled to sit up. "Looks like I've won the grand prize."

Still standing, Maisie froze, locked in horror.

Grimacing, Gambell pointed his gun at her.

Something weighed in Maisie's hand. She glanced down. The muzzleloader. She hiked it up to her shoulder well. The fire behind her provided adequate light to see down the sights. She lined them up.

This was for the lost letters, for kidnapping Cara, and for shooting Christopher and Cyrus. And for threatening her life. She glared through the little Vs.

Gambell's lip curled. "You can't shoot with that thing. Last time you nearly blew up yourself."

Strength flowed through her. Confidence, anger, love—whatever the source, she felt it. "I've learned how to shoot since then." Maisie cocked the hammer and let it go. A shot echoed around. Maisie's ears rang. Sulfur tainted the air.

Gambell dropped with a hand clutched to his chest.

Lowering the muzzleloader, she ran to Cyrus and knelt in the mud, dropping the flintlock. Through the blaze of light coming from the fire, she inspected his body for wounds. Blood bubbled from his right shoulder.

He blinked and opened his eyes and smiled.

Relief washed over her. She grasped him in an embrace. "You're alive! I thought you dead." She knelt over him, not caring about the mud seeping into her skirts.

He cracked a smile. "Greasy was a terrible shot. It's just a scratch."

She stroked his coal-black hair, savoring his face. "You saved my life."

He rose onto an elbow. "My life is yours to command." He reached up and pinched a strand of her hair.

Maisie threaded her hands around his neck. Her heart pounded, ready to explode like that lantern. She closed her eyes and settled her lips onto his.

His lips brushed hers in a tender sweep.

Goose bumps rose on her skin. Soaking in his breath, she breathed him in. Sensations burst through her, filling every empty space within her body. Never had two hearts beat more harmoniously. She surrendered completely. She slid a hand over his scarred cheek.

Cyrus stopped kissing. "Does it offend you?"

"Does what offend me?"

He smiled and kissed her jaw. "Nothing."

Maisie leaned into his embrace and gave him everything.

****

Maisie blinked as dawn crept over the range. Had she fallen asleep for a few hours in Cyrus's arms? Wrapped in his embrace, it was the best sleep she'd ever had. When horse hoofs thundered through the stockyard, Maisie sat up. Taking Cyrus's hand, she smiled wryly. *At last!*

The sheriff and his posse stopped a few paces away.

Sheriff nodded and dismounted. "Hanks found us and sent us this way. About half way here, we ran into Captain Peele. He told us you were facing the gang yourselves. We saw the smoke and figured something went awry."

Men from the posse jumped off the horses and grabbed water buckets to extinguish the smoldering beams of the barn and led the animals away from the smoke and ash.

One man wrapped Maisie in a blanket.

She shivered and watched the scene still in shock.

"Let's see if we can find the money they stole from the train." The sheriff picked through bags on the horses. "Ah, here we are! Gold, cash, and jewelry."

Cyrus searched through the unconscious bodies and recovered most of his guns. Then he searched more bags with his bad arm clutched to his chest. "Maisie."

He held up her silk dress intended for her wedding with the pastor. "My dress!" Although it was wrinkled, it was still in good shape.

"It's a sign." Grinning, he placed it in her hands.

"It sure is." She lifted it to her nose. The dress still smelled of lavender.

"What was the other thing you lost to the bandits?" Cyrus held open a bag.

"Other things?" Maisie tilted her head. "Oh, the letters blew out the window. They are not recoverable."

Cyrus took her hand and kissed it. "I know every word I wrote in those letters. They are not lost. I would gladly spend the rest of my days telling you."

Warmth filtered through her.

The sheriff slapped Cyrus on his good shoulder. "We'll clean up here. You should get home and get some rest. A mighty big reward will be awaiting you for their capture. Thank you so much for helping bring in these ruffians."

Maisie stared at Gambell's body lying on its back. Had she really killed a man? She hugged her silk dress tighter to her body and hid it in the blanket.

Using his boot, Cyrus flipped over the body. "Clean shot right through the heart. Good job." Blood stained Gambell's shirt.

She frowned. "I was aiming for his head."

****

Two weeks later at the boarding house, Maisie tiptoed downstairs in her white silk dress.

Cara, ahead of her, wore Maisie's apricot silk dress she was supposed to wear to the dance.

Christopher stood at the other end of the room near the hurricane lamps by the parlor windows. His brass buttons seemed to glow extra brightly today. A white sling held his left arm.

"Beautiful day for a double wedding." Mrs. Culpepper swiped her red hair along the side of her bun.

"Yes, ma'am, it is." Sweeping across the room in her long train, Maisie held Cara's hands.

Cara beamed. Her skin healed nicely in the last two weeks. When Christopher removed his hat in the sitting room and winked, Cara smiled all the brighter.

Dropping his hat, he embraced the small Irish girl, enveloping her in his large frame. He bent to give her a kiss.

She raised herself up on her tiptoes to return the embrace, wrapping her arms around his neck.

Maisie sighed with a lightness in her heart. They were the perfect couple. Maisie's groom had yet to appear. She bit her lip. He didn't forget, did he? Something must be keeping him. She paced the worn braided rug.

Mrs. Culpepper held up the paper. "Did you see the newsprint this morning?"

"No, I haven't." She crossed the room to read.

Mrs. Culpepper nodded. "Seems you're a national hero. The sheriff recovered nearly all the property and money stolen from the train robbery. Four men are in jail, awaiting trial. It's been an exciting two weeks."

Grinning, Maisie leaned closer to the gas lamp and stared at the article describing her heroic act of capturing the train robbers, complete with the description of the barn fire and shoot-out. This print came from back East. Sure enough, her mother would read this printed paper, if she hadn't already as the date was several days old. Imagine her reaction! Well, at least she'd know Maisie was alive and well. She'd need to write her mother and let her know that she was safe. And to let her grandfather know that she'd taken good care of the gun. It would now have a place of honor across her own mantel. She'd sign the letter Mrs. Haddock. Behind her, a cough sounded.

Cyrus stood in the doorway with his new hat tucked under his good arm. The other hung in a white sling.

Work would have to wait for a while until he healed, which was just fine with Maisie. He was dressed in what was probably his best suit, and honestly, Maisie didn't see anything else, just his eyes full of love for her.

He held out a bouquet of flowers. "Shall we?" He pointed with his hat toward the doorway.

Sun filled the parlor of Mrs. Culpepper's Boarding House.

With a thrill of delight, Maisie snatched the flowers and stepped into the brilliant July sun and into her future.

A word about the author...

Award-winning author, Amey Zeigler received her B.A. in Communication from University of Arizona. When she was nine years old, she started writing romantic mysteries and has been obsessed with the genre ever since. While attending university, she put her studies on hold to live in France and Switzerland for a year and a half. She lives with her husband and three children near Austin, Texas.

http://www.ameyzeigler.com

Other Titles by This Author

August Blues
Baker's Dozen
Summer of Sundaes
Swiss Mistletoe and Macarons
The Swiss Mishap

www.ingramcontent.com/pod-product-compliance
Lightning Source LLC
Chambersburg PA
CBHW070445260626
47161CB00004B/1204